"Not that the story need be long, but it
will take a long while to make it short."
— Henry David Thoreau

D1091676

Leopoldina's Dream

Silvina Ocampo was born in 1906, the youngest of five
daughters. She began her artistic career as a painter, studying
under Giorgio de Chirico and Fernand Léger, but dissatis-
fied with the results she turned to writing. Her stories
appeared in *Sur*, the landmark literary magazine founded by
her sister Victoria, and in 1937 her first short story collection
was published. With Jorge Luis Borges and her husband,
Adolfo Bioy Casares, Silvina Ocampo edited a collection of
fantastic literature, published in 1940, and an anthology of
Argentine poetry which was published the following year.
She has written several volumes of her own poetry and she
was twice awarded the Argentine National Literature Prize.

Daniel Balderston is a professor of Spanish and Latin
American Studies at Tulane University in New Orleans and
is the author of *The Literary Universe of Jorge Luis Borges* and
El precursor velado: R.L. Stevenson en la Obra de Borges. His
translations include *Shadow Play* and *The Rats*, two novellas by
Jose Bianco, and *Goodbyes* by Juan Carlos Onetti, which won
the 1986 Eugene M. Kayden National Translation Award.

Leopoldina's Dream

Silvina Ocampo

Translated by
Daniel Balderston

Penguin Books

PENGUIN BOOKS

Published by the Penguin Group
Penguin Books Canada Ltd., 2801 John Street, Markham, Ontario, Canada L3R 1B4
Penguin Books Ltd., 27 Wrights Lane, London W8 5TZ
Penguin Books, 40 West 23rd Street, New York, New York 10010, U.S.A.
Penguin Books Australia Ltd., Ringwood, Victoria, Australia
Penguin Books (N.Z.) Ltd., 182–190 Wairau Road, Auckland, New Zealand
Penguin Books Ltd., Registered Offices: Harmondsworth, Middlesex, England

First published by Penguin Books Canada Limited, 1988

Canadian Cataloguing in Publication Data
Ocampo, Silvina
Leopoldina's dream
(Penguin short fiction)
Translated from the Spanish.
ISBN 0-14-010011-3
I. Title.   II. Series.
PQ7797.0293A15 1987   869.3′4   C87-093154-7
American Library of Congress Cataloguing in
Publication Data Available

Contents

Preface

Not without some feelings of reticence do I write this preface. An old, yet ever new, friendship binds me to Silvina Ocampo, a friendship based on the shared memory of certain neighbourhoods in Buenos Aires, of sunsets, of walks across the limitless plains or along a river as quiet as the land, of favourite poems: based, above all, on the understanding and kindness that Silvina has never failed to show me. Like Rossetti and Blake, Silvina has come to poetry by the luminous paths of drawing and painting, and the immediacy and certainty of the visual image persist in her written pages.

The range covered by her spirit is much greater than my own. The joys provoked by music and colour, paradises barred to my memory as well as to my curiosity, are familiar to her. I would say the same of the things of nature: flowers, vague names when I come upon them in Latin and Persian verses, signify something precise for Silvina, precise and beloved. The universe I live in is opaque because it is purely verbal; in hers, all the senses take part in their delicate variety. Our literary preferences do not always coincide. I am moved by the epic, she by the lyric and the elegiac; she is not drawn so much to the *Chanson de Roland* and the harsh sagas of Iceland as to Baudelaire, a poet I venerated in my youth, or to the idylls of Theocritus. She also likes the psychological novel, a genre whose slow pace I in my laziness reject.

It is strange that it should be I, for whom telling a story is the attempt to capture only its essential elements, who should present to English readers a work as wise, as changeable, as complex and at the same time as simple as this anthology. I thank the gods for this happy fate.

In Silvina Ocampo's stories there is something I have never understood: her strange taste for a certain kind of innocent and oblique cruelty. I attribute this to the interest, the astonished interest, that evil inspires in a noble soul. The present, we might say in passing, is perhaps no less cruel than the past, or than the various pasts, but its cruelties are clandestine. Gongora, who was a normal man and a fine poet, makes fun of an *auto da fé* performed in Granada because it offered the modest spectacle of only one person burned alive; Hitler, an atrocious man, preferred the anonymous horror of the secret death chambers to the spectacle of public executions. Today cruelty searches out the shadows; cruelty is obscene, in the original meaning of the word.

Silvina has a virtue that is frequently attributed to the ancients and to the peoples of the Orient, and not frequently to our own contemporaries: clairvoyance. More than once, and not without feelings of apprehension, I have noticed it in her. She sees us as if we were made of glass, sees and forgives us. It is useless to try to fool her.

Silvina Ocampo is a poet, one of the greatest poets in the Spanish language, whether on this side of the ocean or on the other. The fact that she is a poet elevates her prose. In the other parts of South America, the short story is usually no more than a simple sketch of daily life or a simple social protest, or often an unhappy mixture of the two; among us, in Argentina, it tends to be the product of an imagination granted the fullest freedom. The book I am introducing is a clear example of this.

Groussac and Alfonso Reyes have renewed the intentionally verbose and sententious Spanish style with the help of the precision of French; Silvina Ocampo has understood their lesson and has constantly improved upon it in magical works.

Jorge Luis Borges

Author's Introduction

Am I an outsider or a liar, a giant or a dwarf, a Spanish dancer or an acrobat? When you write, everything is possible, even the very opposite of what you are. I write so that other people can discover what they should love, and sometimes so they discover what I love. I write in order not to forget what is most important in the world: friendship and love, wisdom and art. A way of living without dying, a way of death without dying. On paper, something of us remains, our soul holds onto something in our lives: something more important than the human voice, which changes with health, luck, muteness and, finally, with age.

What will be left of us in this world? Sentences instead of voices, sentences instead of photographs. I write in order to forget scorn, in order not to forget, in order not to hate, from hate, from love, from memory and so as not to die. Writing is a luxury or, with luck, a rainbow of colours. It is my lifesaver when the water of the river or the sea tries to drag me under. When you want to die you fall in love with yourself, you look for something touching that will save you. I write to be happy or to give happiness. I, who am unhappy for no reason, want to explain myself, to rejoice, to forget, to find something others might find in Ovid in my unhappiness or in my other self.

Palinurus exists in writing, and sleeps in my heart as if in the blue water of the sea. Andersen's mermaid has a beautiful voice I never heard. When I call on the Guardian Angel in my language, he is more beautiful than life itself.

You can perhaps tell the truth by speaking of things of no interest only by not writing. On a white sheet of paper I have been sketching a hand for some time; it is my hand that sketches words. I have loved painting since childhood.

Writing is having a sprite within reach, someone we can turn into a demon or a monster, but also someone who will give us unexpected happiness or the wish to die.

I studied painting with Giorgio di Chirico in Paris. I came to know the trials of artists, and the joys; I submerged myself in colours that reflected my soul or the state of my spirit. Also in Paris, after feeling that Chirico had given me all that he had to give, I went to Leger's academy: an enormous garage converted into a huge hall full of studios, where the students went with their paintings and their canvases, paper and pencils, and where a sad-eyed nude model sat on a platform, waiting for someone to sketch her. There I excelled as a student. Leger congratulated me, but that was not enough for me. I have retained his preference for design, even if his designs are inferior to those of any other painter's. Nothing interested Leger except the design of his paintings, lost among endless colours and brush strokes that no other painter could imitate.

I fought with Giorgio di Chirico and told him he sacrificed everything for the sake of colour. He would answer: "What else is there besides colour?" "You're right. But colour bothers me. You can't see forms in the midst of so many colours."

That is how I started to grow disillusioned. I drew away from a passion that was also a torture for me. What was left for me? Writing? Writing? There was music, but that was as far beyond my reach as the moon. For a long time I had been writing and hiding what I had written. For so long that I suffered from the habit of hiding what I wrote: as if God could heal me and give me a piece of good news that never came. The world is not magical. We make it magical all of a sudden inside us, and nobody finds out until many years later. But I did not hope to be known: that seemed the most horrible thing in the world to me. I will never know what I was hoping for. A beggar who sleeps under a tree without anything in the world to shelter him is happier than a famous man, a man known for his charm, for his talent. What matters is what we write: that is what we are, not some puppet made up by those who talk and enclose us in a prison so different from our dream. Will we always be students of ourselves?

Silvina Ocampo
Buenos Aires

Thus Were Their Faces

Thus were their faces: and their wings were stretched upward; two wings were joined one to another, and two covered their bodies.

Ezekiel 1:11

How did the younger children come to know it? That will never be explained. Besides, one would need to clarify what it was that they came to know, and whether the older ones already knew it. One assumes, nevertheless, that it was a real event, and not a fantasy; only people who did not know them or their school or their teachers could deny it without a qualm.

At the hour when the bell was rung, uselessly, routinely, ritually, to announce the milk or, a little later, during recess, when they ran to the back courtyard: perhaps, as seems most likely, they unconsciously, slowly, constantly, without distinction of age or sex, came to know it, and I say came, because various signs showed that up to that moment they were waiting for something that would allow them to wait once more, and once and for all, for something very important. We know for certain that from then on (from that moment to which I am alluding imprecisely, but which is the subject of thousands of conjectures), without losing their innocence, but losing that apparent

1

nonchalance so characteristic of childhood, the children thought about nothing else.

After long reflection, one can't help but assume that the children discovered it simultaneously. In the dormitories, when they fell asleep; in the dining hall, when they ate; in the chapel, when they prayed; in the courtyards, when they played tag or hopscotch; sitting before their desks, when they did their assignments or were being punished; in the square, when they played on the swings; or in the bathrooms, when they devoted themselves to bodily hygiene (important moments, because during them worries are forgotten), with the same sullen, withdrawn look on their faces, their minds, like little machines, were spinning the web of one sole thought, one sole desire, one sole expectation.

People who saw them going by in their Sunday best, clean and well-groomed, on national or religious holidays, or on any Sunday, would say: "Those children all belong to one family or to one mysterious society. They're identical! Their poor parents! They must not be able to recognize their own children! These modern times, the same barber must cut all their hair (the little girls look like boys and the boys look like girls): cruel, unspiritual times."

In fact, their faces did resemble one another to that degree; they were as lacking in expression as the faces on the badges or the images of the Virgin of Lujan that they wore on their breasts.

But they, each of them, at first felt alone, as if an iron carapace covered them, isolating them, stiffening them. Each one's pain was individual and terrible; their happiness also, which for that very reason was painful. Humiliated, they imagined themselves different from one another, like dogs of various breeds, or like prehistoric monsters in illustrations. They thought that the secret, which was splitting at that very moment into forty secrets, was not shared and would never be shared. But an angel came, the angel who sometimes attends to multitudes; he came with his shining mirror held high, like the picture of the candidate, the hero, or the tyrant that is carried aloft in demonstrations, and showed them that their faces were identical. Forty faces were all the same face; forty minds were all the same mind, despite the differences in ages and families.

No matter how horrible a secret may be, when it is shared it sometimes stops being horrible, because the horror of it gives pleasure: the pleasure of perpetual communication.

But those who suppose it was horrible are jumping ahead. In reality, we don't know whether it was horrible and then became beautiful, or whether it was beautiful and became horrible.

When they felt more sure of themselves, they wrote letters to one another on paper of different colours, with lace borders or pictures pasted on. At first the letters were laconic; later, longer and more confused. They chose strategic places to serve as post offices where the others could pick them up.

Since they were now happy conspirators, the normal difficulties of life no longer troubled them.

If one of them planned to do something, the others immediately resolved to do the same thing.

As if they wanted to become equal, the shorter ones walked on tiptoe so as to look taller; the taller ones stooped over so as to look shorter. One might have said that the redheads reduced the brilliance of their hair and that the darker ones lightened the colour of their warm bronze skin. The eyes all shone with the same brown or grey colour characteristic of light-coloured eyes. Now none of them ever chewed his nails, and the only one who sucked his thumb stopped.

They were also linked by the violence of their gestures, by their simultaneous laughter, by a boisterous and abruptly sad feeling of solidarity that hid in their eyes, in their straight or slightly curly hair. So indissolubly united were they that they would have conquered an army, a pack of hungry wolves, a plague, hunger, thirst, or the earnest exhaustion that destroys civilizations.

At the top of a slide, not from wickedness but from excitement, they almost killed a child who slipped in among them. On the street, in the face of their admiring enthusiasm, a flower vendor almost perished with all his merchandise.

In the dressing rooms, at night, the navy-blue pleated skirts, the pants, the blouses, the rough white underwear, and the handkerchiefs were all crammed together in the darkness, along with that life with which their owners had imbued them during the day. The shoes, all together, ever more together, formed a vigorous, organized army; they walked as much at night without them as they had with them during the day. An unearthly dirt clung to their soles. Shoes are already pathetic enough when they are alone! The bar of soap was passed from hand to hand, from face to face, from chest to chest, acquiring the form of their souls. Bars of soap lost between the toothpaste and the hairbrushes and toothbrushes! All the same!

"One voice is dispersed among those who talk. Those who do not talk transmit its force to the objects that surround them," said Fabia Hernandez, one of the teachers; but neither she, nor Lelia Isnaga, nor Albina Romarin, her colleagues, could penetrate the closed world that sometimes dwells in the heart of a solitary man (who defends and opens himself only to his misfortune or his joy). That closed world dwelt in the heart of forty children! The teachers, who loved their work with utmost devotion, wanted to catch the secret by surprise. They knew that a secret can be poisonous to the soul. Mothers fear the effects it may have on their children; no matter how beautiful it may be, they think, who knows what monsters it may conceal!

They wanted to catch them by surprise. They would suddenly turn on the lights in the bedrooms, under the pretext of needing to inspect the ceiling where a pipe had burst, or because they were hunting down the mice that had invaded the main office; with the excuse of needing to impose silence, they would interrupt the recesses, saying that the racket bothered a sick neighbour or the celebration of a wake; under the pretext of having to do their duty to supervise the religious conduct of the children, they would go into the chapel, where the heightened mysticism allowed for raptures of love in which the children would utter dismembered, but noisy and difficult, words, before the flames of the candles that lit up their hermetic faces.

The children, fluttering like birds, would burst in on the movie theatres or the playhouses of some benefit concert, where they were given the opportunity to entertain or distract themselves with dazzling shows. Their heads turned from right to left, from left to right, all at the same time, revealing the full extent of the pretense.

Miss Fabia Hernandez was the first to notice that the children had the same dreams, that they made the same mistakes in their notebooks, and that when she scolded them for having no personality, they smiled sweetly, something unusual for them.

None of them was troubled by having to suffer for the mischief of a classmate. None of them was troubled when seeing others given credit for his own work.

On various occasions the teachers accused one or two of them of doing assignments for the rest of the students, but it was difficult to explain why the handwriting should be so similar, and the sentences in the compositions so identical. The teachers confirmed that they had been mistaken.

In the drawing class, when the teacher, to stimulate their imagination, asked them to draw any object they felt like, they all, for an alarming length of time, drew wings, the forms and dimensions of which varied infinitely without taking away, according to her, from the monotony of the whole. When they were scolded for always drawing the same thing, they grumbled, and finally wrote on the blackboard, "We feel the wings, Miss."

Without falling into a disrespectful mistake, would it be possible to say they were happy? To the extent that children can be happy, given their limitations, everything leads one to believe that they were, except during the summertime. The heat of the city weighed upon the teachers. At the hour when the children liked to run, climb trees, roll around on the lawn, or go down the hill doing somersaults, all of these amusements were replaced by the siesta, the feared custom of the siesta. The cicadas sang, but the children did not hear that song which makes the heat even more intense. The radios made a racket, but they did not hear that noise which makes the summer, with its sticky asphalt, unbearable.

They wasted hours sitting behind the teachers, who held parasols while waiting for the sun to go down or for the heat to subside. When they were alone they played unintentional pranks like calling some dog from the balcony; when it saw so many possible owners all at once, it would leap madly into the air to reach them. Or, they would whistle at some lady in the street, who would angrily ring the bell to complain of their insolence.

An unexpected donation allowed them all to go on vacation by the sea. The little girls made themselves modest swimsuits; the boys bought theirs at an inexpensive store, where the material smelled of castor oil, but were of a modern cut, one of those that looks good on anybody.

So as to give greater importance to the fact that they would be vacationing for the first time, the teachers, using a pointer, showed them the blue point on the map, by the Atlantic, where they would be going.

They dreamed of the Atlantic, of the sand: all the same dream.

When the train left the station, the handkerchiefs waved back and forth in the train windows like a flock of doves; this is preserved in a picture that appeared in the papers.

When they got to the sea they hardly looked at it; they kept on seeing the sea they had imagined instead of the real one. When they got used to the new landscape, it was difficult to control them. They ran after the foam, which formed drifts similar to those formed by snow. But joy did not make them forget the secret, and they would go gravely back to the rooms, where communication between them was easier. If what they felt was not love, then something very similar to love linked them, gladdened them, exalted them. The older ones, influenced by the younger ones, blushed when the teachers asked them trick questions, and answered with a quick nod. The younger ones, all serious, looked like adults whom nothing could bother. The majority of them had the names of flowers like Jacinto, Dahlia, Daisy, Jasmine, Violet, Rose, Narcissus, Hortense, Camilla: affectionate names chosen by their parents. They carved them in the trunks of trees, with their fingernails, hard as a tiger's; they wrote them on the walls, with gnawed-on pencils; in the sand, with their fingers.

They set off on the trip back to the city, hearts bursting with joy, since they would travel by plane. A film festival was to begin that day, and they caught glimpses of furtive stars at the airport. Their throats hurt from laughing so hard. Their eyes turned bright red from staring.

The news appeared in the papers in texts like this: *The plane in which forty children from a school for deaf-mutes were travelling, on their way back from their first vacation by the sea, suffered an unforeseen accident. A door that came open during the flight caused the disaster. Only the teachers, the pilot and the crew were saved. Miss Fabia Hernandez, when interviewed, assures us that when the children threw themselves into the void they had wings. She wanted to stop the last one, who pulled himself from her arms in order to follow the others like an angel. The scene astonished her so much because of its intense beauty that at first she could not consider it a disaster, but rather a celestial vision she will never forget. She still does not believe in the children's disappearance.*

"God would be playing a mean trick on us if he showed us Heaven while casting us into Hell," declares Miss Lelia Isnaga. "I don't believe in the disaster."

Albina Romarin says, "It was all a dream the children had, wanting to astonish us, just as they did on the swings in the square. Nobody will persuade me they have vanished."

Neither the red sign announcing that the house where the school was located is up for rent, nor the closed blinds, dishearten Fabia Hernandez. With her colleagues, to whom she is linked as the children were linked among themselves, she visits the old building; there she contemplates the students' names written on the walls (inscriptions for which they were punished), and some wings drawn with childish skill, which bear witness to the miracle.

Lovers

In his plastic billfold he carried a picture of her dressed as a harem girl. She had a picture of him, in the uniform of a conscript, on her bedside table.

Their families, jobs, the schedule of meals and bedtimes, conspired so that they could see each other very seldom, but those sporadic meetings were rituals and always took place in wintertime. First they would buy pastries, and then, sitting under the trees, they would savour them, as children do when they take along a snack.

Uncertainty is a form of happiness that works in favour of lovers. Through the labyrinths of their days, of crackly, seemingly endless phone calls, they would always choose the Dahlias Bakery as their meeting place, and always choose Sunday as the day, after discarding other possibilities. Instead of a coat she wore a shaggy plaid blanket, which would come in very handy. By the bakery window they would exchange greetings without looking at each other, making a show of their confusion. Those who don't see each other often don't know what to say: that much is certain.

"Perhaps in a very dark room or in a very fast car," he thought, "I would overcome my shyness." "Perhaps I would know what to say to him in a movie theatre after the intermission, or while taking part in a procession," she thought.

After this internal dialogue, they went into the bakery, the same as always, and bought pieces of four different kinds of cake. One looked like the Monument to the Spaniards, cluttered with plumes of whipped cream and glazed fruit in the form of flowers; another looked like mysterious and very dark lace, with shiny decorations of chocolate and yellow meringue, covered with sprinkles; another looked like a broken marble pedestal, less beautiful than the others but larger, with coffee, whipped cream and pieces of nuts; another looked like part of a coffer, with jewels inlaid in either end and snow on top. After paying, when the package was ready, they went to the Recoleta, next to the wall of the Old Age Home, where children hide after breaking the street lights and beggars go to wash their clothes in the fountains. Next to a frail tree, whose branches act as swings and horses for the children who jump around in them, they sat down on the grass. She opened the package and took out the cardboard tray where the cream and meringue and chocolate glowed, already a bit squashed. Simultaneously, as if they projected their movements on each other (mysterious and subtle mirror!), first with one hand, then with both hands together, they picked up the slices of the cake with plumes of whipped cream (a miniature Monument to the Spaniards), and brought them to their mouths. They chewed in unison and finished swallowing each bite at the same time. With the same surprising harmony they cleaned their fingers on papers that others had left lying on the grass. The repetition of these movements put them in touch with eternity.

After finishing the first slice they once again contemplated the remaining slices on the cardboard tray. With loving greed and greater intimacy they took the second pieces: the slices of chocolate decorated with meringue. Without hesitating, squint-eyed, they lifted them up to mouths that waited wide open. Baby pigeons open their beaks the same way to receive the food brought them by their mothers. With greater energy and speed, but with identical pleasure, they began chewing and swallowing once more, like two gymnasts exercising at the same time. She, from time to time, would turn to watch some passing car especially valuable because it smelled excessively of gasoline or because of its size, or would lift her head to watch a dove, the symbol of love, fluttering clumsily among the branches. He would look forward, perhaps savouring the taste of those treats less consciously than she. The abundant whipped cream dripped on the grass, on the folded blanket, and on some bits of trash nearby. No smile would light up those harmonious lips until they could finish the contents of the little tray of yellowish cardboard covered with waxed paper. The last bit of that piece of cake crumbled between thumb and index finger and took a long time to reach their waiting mouths. The crumbs that fell on the tray, her skirt, and his pants were carefully picked up and lifted with thumb and finger to their lips.

The third slice of cake, even more opulent than the others, looked like the material used to build some of the older houses in beach resorts. The fourth piece, lighter but more difficult to eat because of its sponge-like consistency (coated with sugar), left them with white moustaches and white spots on their lips. They had to stick out their tongues and close their eyes to put it in their mouths. If you didn't dare to take a large bite you missed the best part of the cake, which was covered with peanuts disguised as walnuts or almonds. She stretched out her neck and lowered her head; he did not change his position. The chewing followed a regular rhythm, as if timed with a metronome.

They knew there were other treats left on the cardboard tray. After that first difficult moment, the rest was easy. They used their hands like spoons. Instead of chewing, before swallowing they filled their mouths with cream and sponge cake.

After they had finished the contents of the tray, she tossed off the festooned cardboard and took a little package of peanuts out of her pocket. For several minutes, with the studied gestures of a model, she opened the shells, peeled the nuts, and gave them to him; she saved some for herself, putting them in her mouth and chewing in unison with him. Licking their lips they attempted a shy conversation on the theme of picnics: people who had died after drinking wine or eating watermelon; a poisonous spider in a picnic basket that killed a girl much loathed by her in-laws one Sunday; canned goods gone bad, but seemingly delicious, which caused the death of two families in Trenque Lauquen; a storm in which two couples drowned while celebrating their honeymoons with hard cider and rolls with sausages on the banks of a stream in Tapalque.

When they had finished the food and the conversation, she unfolded the blanket and they covered themselves with it, lying on the grass. They smiled for the first time, their mouths full of food and words, but she knew (and he did too) that, under the cover of that blanket, love would repeat its usual actions, and that hope, farther and farther off on fickle wings, would draw her away from marriage.

Revelation

Whether he opened his mouth or not, people guessed the inevitable truth from the way he looked: Valentin Brumana was an idiot. He used to say: "I'm going to marry a star."

"Sure, he's going to marry a star," we would answer to make him suffer.

We enjoyed torturing him. We'd make him lie in a hammock, then we'd tie the sides together so he couldn't escape, and rock him back and forth till he got so dizzy he would close his eyes. We would make him get on the swings, roll up the ropes on either side, then let them go all at once and push him off dizzily into space. We didn't let him taste the desserts we ate, but would rub sweets or sticky sugar in his hair and make him cry. We put the toys he asked to borrow on top of a tall chest; to reach them he would climb unsteadily on a wobbly table with two chairs piled on one another, one of them a rocker.

When we discovered that Valentin Brumana, without making any show of it, was a sort of magician, we began to have a little respect for him, maybe even fear.

"Did you see your girlfriend tonight?" he would say to us. That evening we had met one of our girlfriends on the sly in a vacant lot. We were so precocious!

"Who are you hiding from?" he would ask us. It was the day we got report cards full of bad grades, and we were hiding because our father was looking for us to punish us, or to give us a sermon, which was a thousand times worse.

"You're sad, with a mournful face," he would exclaim. He said it at the very moment we wanted to kill ourselves out of sorrow, of a sorrow we concealed like our dates with our girlfriends.

Valentin Brumana's life was full of excitement, not only because of what we did to him but also because of his intense activity. He had a pocket watch his uncle had given him. It was a real watch, not made of chocolate or tin or plastic, as he really deserved, according to us; I think it was made of silver, and the chain had a little medal of the Virgin of Lujan. The sound the watch made banging against the medal, each time he took it out of his pocket, demanded respect, as long as we didn't look at the watch's owner, who made you laugh. A thousand times a day he would take the watch out of his pocket and say: "I have to go to work." He would get up and abruptly leave the room; then he would come right back.

Nobody paid any attention to him. They gave him old records, old magazines to amuse him.

When he worked as a scribe, he would use toilet paper, if that's all he could find, pencils and a broken briefcase; when he worked as an electrician, the same briefcase would be used as a toolbox to carry insulating tape and wire, which he would collect in the garbage; when he worked as a carpenter, a wash rack, a broken bench and a hammer were his tools; when he worked as a photographer, I would lend him my camera, without any film in it. Nonetheless, if anyone asked him, "Valentin, what are you going to be when you grow up?" he would answer, "A priest or a waiter." "Why?" we would ask. "Because I like to clean silver."

One day Valentin Brumana woke up with a fever. The doctors said, in a roundabout way, that he was going to die and that, considering what his life was like, perhaps it was for the best. He was there and heard those words without alarm, though they shook the whole desolate house, since at that moment the entire family, even we, his cousins, thought that Valentin Brumana made people happy because he was so different, and that in his absence he would be irreplaceable.

Death didn't keep us waiting long. The next morning she arrived:

everything makes me think that Valentin in his agony saw her come in the door to his room. The joy of greeting a beloved person lit up his face, which usually expressed indifference. He stretched out his arm and pointed a finger at her.

"Come in," he said. Then, looking at us out of the corner of his eye, he exclaimed, "How lovely!"

"Who? Who's lovely?" we asked him, with a daring that now seems rude to me. We laughed, but our laughter could easily be confused with crying: tears poured from our eyes.

"This lady," he said, blushing.

The door had opened. My cousin assures me that that door always opened by itself, because the lock was broken, but I don't believe her. Valentin sat up in bed and greeted the apparition we couldn't see. It's clear beyond a doubt that he saw her, that he touched the veil that hung from her shoulder, that she whispered some secret to him that we would never hear. Then, something even more unusual happened: with a great deal of effort Valentin gave me the camera that had been lying on his night table and asked me to take a picture of them. He showed his companion how to pose.

"No, don't sit like that," he said to her.

Or instead, in a whisper, almost inaudible: "The veil, the veil is hiding your face."

Or instead, in an authoritarian tone: "Don't look off the other way."

The whole family, and some of the servants, laughing loudly, raised the velvet drapes, which were tall and heavy, so that more light would come in; someone paced out the number of metres that separated the camera from Valentin, so that the picture would not be out of focus. Trembling, I focused on Valentin, who pointed to the place, more important than he, a little to the left, which should also be in the picture: an empty space. I obeyed.

Soon thereafter I had the film developed. Of the six photographs, I thought they had given me one by mistake, one taken by some other amateur. Nonetheless, Pygmy, my pony, came out clear enough; Tapioca, Facundo's puppy, did too; the baker bird's nest was recognizable, though a bit dark and blurry; as for the one of Gilberta, in a bathing suit, well, it could have been entered in any photo contest, even today; also, the picture of the façade of the school, to mention just one, could have been used as a photogravure in *La Nacion*. I had taken all those snapshots that same week.

At first I didn't look too hard at the blurry unknown photograph. Indignant, I went to the lab to protest, but they assured me they had not made a mistake and that it must have been some snapshot taken by one of my little brothers.

It was only somewhat later and after careful study that I was able to make out the room, the furniture, and Valentin's blurry face in the famous photograph. The central figure—clear, terribly clear—was that of a woman covered with veils and scapularies, a bit old already and with big hungry eyes, who turned out to be Pola Negri.

The Fury

Sometimes I think I can still hear that drum. How can I leave this place without being seen? And, supposing I were able to leave, once I was outside, how would I be able to take the child home? I would hope someone would place ads on the radio or in the newspaper searching for him. Make him disappear? Impossible. Kill myself? That would be the last resort. Besides, by what means? Escape? By what route? Right now, the hallways are full of people. The windows are walled up.

I asked myself these questions a thousand times before noticing the penknife the child was holding in his hand, which he sometimes put in his pocket. I calmed down, thinking that if all else failed I could kill him, cutting the veins of his wrists in the bathtub so as not to soil the floor. Once he was dead I would stuff him under the bed.

So that I wouldn't go crazy I took out the notebook I always carry in my pocket, and while the child, strangely, played with the fringe of the bedspread, with the rug, with the chair, I wrote down everything that had happened to me since I met Winifred.

I met her in Palermo Park. Her eyes glistened, I now realize, like a hyena's. She reminded me of one of the Furies. She was fragile and nervous, like all the women you don't like, Octavio. Her black hair was curly and fine, like armpit hair. I never found out what perfume she

used, since her natural odour altered that of the unlabelled bottle
decorated with Cupids I glimpsed in the disorder of her purse.

Our first dialogue was brief:

"Sweetheart, you don't look like you're from here, from Argentina."

"Of course not. I'm Filipina."

"Do you speak English?"

"Of course."

"You could teach me."

"Why?"

"It would help me with my studies."

She was walking with a child she was taking care of: I, with a math or
logic book under my arm. Winifred was not especially young; I could
tell that from the veins on her legs, which formed little blue trees
behind her knees, and from her swollen eyelids. She told me she was
twenty.

I saw her on Saturday afternoons. For a while, we would follow the
same path we had the first day, walking from the bust of Dante by a
terebinth tree up to the monkey house. We would stare at the tips of
our shoes covered with dust, or feed raw meat to the cats; we would
repeat the same dialogue, with different emphases, one might almost
say with different meanings. The child banged constantly on his
drum. We tired of the cats the first day we held hands: we no longer
had time to cut up so many little pieces of raw meat. One day I took
bread for the pigeons and swans: this served as a pretext for a picture
taken at the foot of the bridge that goes over to the little walled island
in the middle of the lake, the gate covered with pornographic inscriptions. She wanted me to write her name and mine next to one of the
most obscene messages. I obeyed her reluctantly.

I fell in love with her the day she spoke in verse (Octavio, you taught
me everything about metrics).

"I remember my angel wings as a child."

So as not to upset myself, I looked at her reflection in the water. I
thought she was crying.

"You had angel wings?" I asked in a sentimental voice.

"They were made of cotton and were very large," she answered.
"They framed my face. They looked as if they were made of ermine.
For the Virgin Mary's day, the nuns at the school dressed me as an
angel in a light-blue dress; a tunic, not a dress. Underneath I wore

light-blue tights and shoes. They made me curls and pasted them on."

I put my arm around her waist, but she kept on talking.

"On my head they put a crown of artificial lilies. A very fragrant kind of lily, tuberose I believe. Yes, tuberose. I threw up all night long. I'll never forget that day. My friend Lavinia, who was as well-liked at the school as I was, received the same distinction: they dressed her as an angel, as a pink angel. (The pink angel was less important than the blue angel.)"

(I remembered your advice, Octavio: there's no need to be shy when seducing a woman.)

"Don't you want to sit down?" I said to her, taking her in my arms, in front of a marble bench.

"Let's sit on the grass," she said to me.

She took a few steps and threw herself down on the ground.

"I'd like to find a four-leaf clover ... and I'd like to give you a kiss."

She went on, as if she hadn't heard me: "My friend Lavinia died that day; it was the happiest and the saddest day of my life. Happy, because the two of us were dressed as angels; sad, because that day I lost happiness forever."

I put my hand on her cheek to touch her tears.

"Every time I remember her, I cry," she said, her voice cracking. "That festive day ended in tragedy. One of Lavinia's wings got caught in the flame of a tall candle I was holding in my hand. Lavinia's father rushed over to save his daughter: he picked her up, ran to the chancel, crossed the patio, went into the bathroom with that living torch. When he put her in the water in the bathtub it was already too late. My friend Lavinia lay there in cinders. All that was left of her body was this ring I guard as if it were gold dust," she told me, showing me a little ruby ring on her third finger. "One day, when we were playing, she promised me the ring when she died. There were, of course, schemers who accused me of having set Lavinia's wings on fire on purpose. The truth is that I can only take pride in having been good to one person in my life: to her. I devoted myself like a mother to taking care of her, educating her, correcting her faults. We all have faults: Lavinia was proud and fearful. She had long blond hair and very white skin. One day, to correct her pride, I cut off a lock of her hair, putting it away secretly in a locket; they had to cut the rest of her hair to even it out. Another day I spilled a bottle of cologne on her neck and cheek; her skin got all stained."

The child was playing the drum next to us. We told him to go off somewhere, but he didn't obey us.

"And if we were to take away his drum?" I asked impatiently.

"He would have a fit," Winifred answered me.

"May I see you some time without the child or without the drum?"

"Not for the moment," answered Winifred.

I even came to believe that he was her child, she spoiled him so.

"And his mother, his mother can't ever be with him?" I asked her one day, bitterly.

"That's what they pay me for," she answered, as if I had insulted her.

After several kisses, exchanged amidst the foliage, she continued with her confidences, though the child didn't stop playing the drum even for a moment.

"In the Philippines there are paradises."

"Here too," I answered, thinking she was talking of a kind of tree.

"Paradises of happiness. In Manila, where I was born, the windows of the houses were decorated with mother-of-pearl."

"Can one achieve happiness with windows decorated with mother-of-pearl?"

"Being in paradise is achieving happiness; but the serpent is always on its way, and one always awaits it. The earthquakes, the Japanese invasion, Lavinia's death, all that happened later. Nonetheless, I had premonitions. My parents always put out a bowl of milk for the snakes just outside our house, by the front door, so they wouldn't come in. One night they forgot to put the milk outside. When my father got in bed, he felt something cold between the sheets. It was a snake. He had to wait till the next morning before shooting it. He didn't want to scare us with the noise. That time I foresaw everything that was going to happen. It was a premonition. Kneeling in the chapel at school I tried to ask for God's protection, but every time I knelt down my feet bothered me. I would turn them in and out, put them on one side, then on the other, without being able to find a posture that would allow contemplation. Lavinia looked at me with astonishment; she was very intelligent and could not understand that one could have these difficulties before God. She was sensible; I was romantic. One day, while reading in a field of irises, I fell asleep. It was late. They looked for me with flashlights; the group was led by Lavinia. There the irises make you sleepy; they're narcotic. If they hadn't found me, you'd certainly not be talking to me today."

The child sat down next to us, playing his drum.

"Why don't we take his drum away from him and throw it in the lake?" I dared to suggest. "The noise is driving me crazy."

Winifred folded her red raincoat, stroked it and went on talking: "In the dormitories at the school, Lavinia would cry at night because she was afraid of animals. To combat her inexplicable terror, I would put live spiders in her bed. Once I put a dead rat that I found in the garden; another time I put a toad. Despite all my efforts I didn't succeed in correcting her; quite the contrary, her fear got worse for a while. It reached a climax the day I invited her to my house. Around the little table where the tea set was arranged with the pastries, I put the beasts my father had hunted in Africa and had stuffed: two tigers and a lion. Lavinia didn't try the milk or the pastries that day. I pretended to give food to the animals. She didn't stop crying until nightfall. Then I took advantage of the darkness to hide behind some plants. Fear dried her tears. She thought she was alone. The place where the hammocks were was some distance from the house. She stood there, next to a rough bench, nervously scratching her knees, until I appeared covered with banana leaves. In the darkness I could guess the pallor of her face and the two little lines of blood on her scratched knees. I cried out her name three times: "Lavinia, Lavinia, Lavinia," trying to alter my voice. I touched her icy hand. I believe she fainted. That night they had to put hot water bottles on her feet and bags of ice on her head. Lavinia told her parents that she didn't want to see me ever again. We were later reconciled, as was to be expected. To celebrate our reconciliation, I went to her house with several gifts: chocolate and a fish bowl with a goldfish; but the gift that Lavinia found most unpleasant was a little monkey, dressed in green, with four bells on. Lavinia's parents received me affectionately and thanked me for the presents, but Lavinia didn't thank me for them. I believe the fish and the monkey starved to death. As for the chocolate, Lavinia never tried it. She disliked sweets, something they scolded her for; sometimes they would even force the candies or sweets I always gave her as presents down her throat."

"Don't you want to go somewhere else?" I asked, interrupting her confidences. "It's raining."

"All right," she answered, putting on her raincoat.

We walked, crossed the avenue lined with palm trees, reached the Monument to the Spaniards. We looked for a taxi. I gave directions to the chauffeur. On the way we bought chocolate and bread for the child. The house was like others of the same kind, perhaps a bit larger. The room had a mirror with a gold frame and a clothes rack; the hangers had designs of swan necks on them. We hid the drum under the bed.

"What shall we do with the child?" I asked. The only answer I got was the embrace that led us into a labyrinth of other embraces. We went in, pausing in the darkness as if in a tunnel, still blinded by the light of the garden we had just left.

"And the child?" I asked again, seeing that he was not there, seeing the straw hat and white gloves there in the twilight. "Could he be under the bed?"

"That ragamuffin must be walking around the hallways."

"And if someone sees him?"

"They'll think he's the owner's kid."

"How come they let him in?"

"They didn't see him under your raincoat."

I closed my eyes and smelled Winifred's perfume.

"How cruel you were to Lavinia," I told her.

"Cruel, cruel?" she answered emphatically. "I'm cruel to everyone. I'll be cruel to you," she said, biting my lips.

"You can't."

"You're sure?"

"I'm sure."

I now understand she wanted to redeem herself for what she had done to Lavinia by committing still greater cruelties with everyone else. To redeem herself through evil.

I went out looking for the child, as she asked me to. I wandered around the hallways. There wasn't anyone there. I stood by the terrace where the taxis came with couples who tried to hide their laughter, their joy, their shame. A white cat climbed up a vine. The child was peeing by a wall. I picked him up and carried him back with me, hiding him as best I could. When I entered the room, I couldn't see anything at first; it was pitch dark. Then I saw that Winifred was not there any more. Nor were her things; her purse, her gloves, nor her scarf with light-blue initials. I ran to open the door to see if I could spot her down the hall, but I couldn't even smell her perfume. I closed the door again, and while the child played in a dangerous fashion with the fringes of the bedspread, I found the drum. I went through all the corners where the absent-minded Winifred might have left something of hers that would help me find her again: her address, the address of some friend, her last name.

I tried several times to talk to the child, but it was not much use.

"Don't play the drum. What's your name?"

"Cintito."

"That's your nickname. What's your real name?"

"Cintito."

"And your nursemaid?"

"Nana."

"Where does she live?"

"In a little house."

"Where?"

"In a little house."

"Where is that little house?"

"I don't know."

"I'll give you some candy if you tell me your nursemaid's name."

"Give me some candy."

"Later. What's her name?"

Cintito kept playing with the bedspread, with the rug, with the chair, with the drumsticks.

What should I do? I thought, as I talked to the child.

"Don't play the drum. It's more fun to roll it."

"Why?"

"Because it's better not to make noise."

"But I want to."

"I told you not to."

"Then give me my penknife back."

"It's not a toy for children. You could hurt yourself."

"I'm going to play the drum."

"If you play the drum, I'll kill you."

He started screaming. I took him by the neck. I asked him to be quiet. He refused to listen to me. I covered his mouth with the pillow. He struggled for a few minutes; then he lay still, his eyes closed.

Vacillation is one of my faults. During several minutes that were my first experience of eternity, I repeated over and over: What shall I do?

Now I can only wait for the door of this cell to open. That's how I was: to avoid a scandal, I was capable of committing a crime.

The Photographs

I arrived with my presents. I greeted Adriana. She was sitting in the middle of the patio in a wicker chair, surrounded by the guests. She was wearing a very full, white organdy skirt over a starched petticoat (the lace hem peeking out at the slightest movement), and had a metal clasp with white flowers in her hair, leather orthopedic bootees, and a pink fan in her hand. That vocation for misfortune which I had discovered in her long before the accident was not evident in her face.

Clara, Rossi, Cordero, Perfecto and Juan were all there, along with Albina Renato, Maria, the one with the glasses, that nitwit Acevedo with his new teeth, the deceased's three boys, a blond boy nobody introduced to me, and that wretch Humberta. Luqui was there, and little Dwarf, and the kid who used to be Adriana's boyfriend but who didn't talk to her any more. I was shown the presents: they were arranged on a shelf in the bedroom. The table, which was very long, had been set under a yellow canopy in the courtyard; it was covered with two tablecloths. The sandwiches of ham and vegetables and the beautifully decorated cakes whetted my appetite. Half a dozen bottles of sparkling cider, and the glasses to go with them, glittered on the table. It all made my mouth water. A vase with orange gladioli and another with white carnations decorated either end of the table. We were awaiting the arrival of Spirito, the photographer: we were not to sit down at the table, to open the bottles of cider, nor to taste the cakes, until he arrived.

To make us laugh, Albina Renato danced "The Death of the Swan." She studies classical ballet, but danced in a spirit of fun.

It was hot and there were lots of flies. The flowers of the catalpa trees stained the tiles of the patio. All the guests fanned themselves, the men with their newspapers, the women with improvised shades or fans, or they fanned the cakes and sandwiches. That wretch Humberta fanned herself with a flower to attract attention. No matter how much you wave it back and forth, how much breeze can you stir up with a flower?

We waited around for an hour, asking ourselves each time the doorbell rang whether Spirito was coming or not, and entertaining ourselves with stories of more-or-less fatal accidents. Some of the victims had been left without arms, others without hands, others without ears. "The misfortune of the many is the consolation of the few," said a little old lady, referring to Rossi, who has a glass eye. Adriana smiled. The guests kept arriving. When Spirito came in, the first bottle of cider was opened. Of course nobody tried it yet. Various glasses were served and the long prelude to the long-awaited toast began.

In the first photograph, Adriana, at the head of the table, tried to smile with her parents. It was very hard to arrange the group right, since it didn't blend easily: Adriana's father was robust and very tall, and the parents knitted their brows very noticeably while holding their glasses aloft. The second photograph wasn't any easier: the younger brothers and sisters, the aunts, and the grandmother clustered around Adriana in disorder, blocking her face. Poor Spirito had to wait patiently for a moment of calm, when all of them took the places he had assigned them. In the third photograph Adriana brandished the knife to cut the cake, which had her name, her birthday, and the word "Happiness" written on it in pink icing, and was covered with sprinkles.

"She should stand up," the guests said.

An aunt objected: "And if her feet come out wrong?"

"Don't worry," responded the friendly Spirito. "If her feet come out wrong I'll cut them off later."

Adriana grimaced with pain, and once more poor Spirito had to take her picture sunken in her chair amidst the guests. In the fourth photograph, only the children surrounded Adriana; they were allowed to hold their glasses high in imitation of the adults. The children caused less trouble than the adults. The most difficult moment still remained. Adriana had to be carried off to her grandmother's bedroom for the last photographs to be taken. Two men carried her in her wicker chair and put her in the room, along with the gladioli and the carnations. They sat her down on a couch, between piles of pillows. There must have been about fifteen people in the bedroom, which measured fifteen by twenty feet; they all drove poor Spirito crazy, giving him directions and telling Adriana how she should pose. They fixed her hair, covered her feet, added pillows, arranged flowers and fans, raised her head, buttoned her collar, powdered her nose, painted her lips. You couldn't even breathe. Adriana sweated and grimaced. Poor Spirito waited for more than half an hour without saying a word; then, with a great deal of tact, he took away the flowers they had put around Adriana's feet, saying that the girl was dressed in white and that the orange gladioli did not go with the ensemble. Patiently, Spirito repeated the well-known command: "Watch the birdie."

He turned on the lamps and took the fifth photograph, which ended in a thunder of applause. From outside, people said: "She looks like a bride, like a real bride. What a shame about the bootees."

Adriana's aunt asked that they take a picture of the girl holding the aunt's mother-in-law's fan. It was a fan of Alençon lace and sequins, decorated with little pictures painted by hand on the mother-of-pearl ribs. Poor Spirito did not think it in good taste to introduce a sad black fan, no matter how valuable it might be, into the picture of a fourteen-year-old girl. They insisted so much that he gave in. With a white carnation in one hand and the black fan in the other, Adriana appeared in the sixth photograph. The seventh photograph stirred up much debate: whether it should be taken inside the room or on the patio, next to Adriana's cranky grandfather who did not want to move from his corner. Clara said: "If this is the happiest day of her life, how can you fail to take her picture with her grandfather, who loves her so much!" Then she explained: "For a year this girl has been hovering between life and death, ending up paralyzed."

The aunt declared: "We've been killing ourselves to save her, sleeping by her side on the tile floors of the hospitals, giving our blood for transfusions. And now, on her birthday, are we to neglect the most solemn moment of the banquet, and forget to put her in the most important group of all, next to the grandfather who was always her favourite?"

Adriana was complaining. I think she was asking for a glass of water, but she was so upset she couldn't utter a single word; besides, the racket people made when they moved around and talked would have drowned out her words even if she had uttered them. Two men carried her, once more, in the wicker chair to the patio, and put her at the table. At this moment the traditional song "Happy Birthday" was heard over a loudspeaker. Adriana, sitting at the head of the table, by her grandfather and the cake covered with candles, posed for the seventh photograph with great serenity. That wretch Humberta managed to slip into the front of the picture, with her shoulders and breasts showing as always. I accused her in public of butting in and advised the photographer to take the picture over, which he did willingly enough. Resentful, that wretch Humberta went into a corner of the patio; the blond boy nobody had introduced to me followed her and, to console her, whispered something in her ear. If it had not been for that wretch the catastrophe wouldn't have happened. Adriana was about to faint when they took her picture again. Everybody thanked me. They opened the bottles of cider; the glasses overflowed with foam. They cut the two cakes in big slices that were handed around on plates. These things took time and attention. Some glasses were spilled on the tablecloth; they say that brings good luck. With our fingertips we moistened our brows. Some people with no manners had already drunk their cider before the toast. That wretch Humberta set the example, and passed her cup on to the blond boy. It wasn't until later, when we tasted the cake and toasted Adriana's health, that we noticed she was asleep. Her head hung down from her neck like a melon. Since this was her first day out of the hospital, it was not odd that exhaustion and emotion should have overcome her. Some people laughed; others approached her and clapped her on the back to wake her up. That wretch Humberta, that party-pooper, jostled her by the arm and cried out to her: "You're frozen."

Then that bird of ill omen said: "She's dead."

Some people at a distance from the head of the table thought it was a joke and said: "Who wouldn't burst with happiness on such a day!"

That nitwit Acevedo didn't let go of his glass. Everyone stopped eating except Luqui and Dwarf. Others, on the sly, slipped pieces of squashed cake without icing into their pockets.

How unfair life is! Instead of Adriana, who was an angel, that wretch Humberta might have died!

The Clock House

Dear Miss ———:

   Since I have always excelled in your classes with my compositions, I will keep my word: I will practise by writing letters to you. You ask what I did during the last few days of my vacation.

   As I write to you, Joaquina is snoring. It's nap time and as you know at this hour and at night Joaquina, because she has a fleshy nose, snores more than usual. It's too bad because she doesn't let anybody sleep. I am writing to you in my notebook from school because the letter paper I got from Pituco doesn't have lines on it and my writing goes all over the place. The puppy Julia is asleep now under my bed; she cries when moonlight comes in the window, but that doesn't matter to me because even Joaquina's snoring doesn't wake me up.

   We went for an excursion to the Salada Lagoon. Swimming is wonderful. I sank up to my knees in the mud. I gathered herbs for the herbarium and also, in the trees that were some distance away, gathered eggs for my collection: ringdove, magpie and partridge eggs. The partridges don't lay their eggs in the trees but on the ground, poor things. I had a great time at the lagoon—we made mud castles— but I had even more fun last night at the party Ana Maria Sausa gave for little Rusito's baptism. The whole patio was decorated with paper lanterns and streamers. They set four tables, made out of boards and sawhorses, with all kinds of food and drink; it made you hungry just looking at it. They didn't have hot chocolate because of the milk strike and because my father gets excited just at the sight of it and it's bad for his liver.

That day, Estanislao Romagan put aside the pile of clocks he was working on to see how the preparations for the party were coming along and to help out a little (he who even on Sundays and holidays never stops working). I was very fond of Estanislao Romagan. Do you remember that hunchbacked watchmaker who fixed your clock? The one who lived on the flat roof of this building in the little hut he built himself, which looked like a dog house? I called it the Clock House. The one who specialized in alarm clocks? Who knows, maybe you've forgotten him, though I can hardly believe that! Watches and hunchbacks can't be forgotten just like that. Well, that was Estanislao Romagan. He would show me pictures of a sun dial that shot off cannons automatically at noon; of another one, not a sun dial, that looked like a fountain on the outside; and of another, the Edinburgh clock, with a stairway, cars and horses, figures of women in tunics, and strange little men. You'll hardly believe me, but it was wonderful to hear the different noises of all the alarm clocks going off all the time and the clocks marking the hour a thousand times a day. My father did not agree. For the party, Estanislao pulled out a suit he had stored in a little trunk between two ponchos, a blanket, and three pairs of shoes that belonged to someone else. The suit was wrinkled, but Estanislao, after washing his face and combing his hair, which is very shiny and black and reaches almost to his eyebrows like a Spanish beret, looked quite elegant.

"Sitting down, with your head resting on the pillow, you will look very good. You have a good bearing, better than that of most of the guests," my mother commented.

"Let me touch your back," said Joaquina, running around the house after him.

He let her touch his back because he was very kind.

"And who will bring me good luck?" he said.

"You're a lucky man," responded Joaquina; "you have all the luck in the world."

But to me it seemed unfair to say that to him. What do you think, Miss?

The party was wonderful. Whoever says different is a liar. Pirucha danced rock and roll and Rosita danced Spanish dances, which she does well even though she is a blonde.

We ate club sandwiches already a bit dry, pink meringues that tasted like perfume, the little tiny ones, and cake and candies. The drinks were delicious. Pituco mixed them, shook them, and served them like a real waiter in a restaurant. Everybody gave me a little of this, a little of that, and that way I was able to come up with about three glassfuls altogether, at the very least.

Iriberto asked me: "Hey, kid, how old are you?"

"Nine."

"Did you have anything to drink?"

"No, not even a sip," I answered, because I was ashamed.

"Well, then, have this glass."

And he made me drink something that burned my throat all the way down. He laughed and said: "That way you will be a man."

It's not right to do these things to a child, don't you think, Miss?

People were very jolly. My mother, who hardly ever talks, was chattering away with some woman or another, and Joaquina who is shy danced by herself, singing a Mexican song she did not know by heart. I, who am so unsociable, even talked with the mean old man who always tells me to go to hell. It had gotten late by the time Estanislao finally came down from his hut all dressed and brushed, apologizing for his wrinkled suit. They gave him a round of applause and something to drink. They paid him lots of attention, offering him the best sandwiches, the best sweets, the tastiest drinks. One girl, the prettiest one, I think, in the whole party, picked a flower from a vine and stuck it in his buttonhole. I'd say he was king of the party; he got happier and happier with each drink. The ladies showed him watches that were broken or didn't work right, though they all wore them on their wrists nonetheless. He looked at them smiling, promising to fix them at no charge. He apologized again for wearing such a wrinkled suit and said with a laugh that it was because he wasn't used to going to parties. Then Gervasio Palmo, who has a laundry around the corner, came up to him and said: "Let's iron it right away in my laundry. What are laundries for if not to press the suits of our friends?"

Everyone welcomed the idea enthusiastically. Even Estanislao himself, who is a very moderate man, cried with joy and danced a few steps in time with the music from a radio placed in the middle of the patio. That's how the pilgrimage to the laundry started. My mother, sad because they had broken the prettiest knick-knack in the house and had messed up a macrame rug, held my arm: "Don't go, sweetheart. Help me clean things up."

Paying as much attention as if the cat had spoken to me (though you may not believe me), I went running after Estanislao, Gervasio and the rest of the group. Except for Estanislao's clock house my favourite place in the neighbourhood is LA MANCHA LAUNDRY. Inside there are hat blocks, huge irons, things with steam coming out of them, gigantic bottles, and a fish tank in the window with goldfish in it. Gervasio Palmo's partner, whom we call Nakoto, is Japanese, and the fish tank belongs to him. Once he gave me a little plant, but it died two days later. How could he expect a kid to like a plant? Those things are for grownups, don't you think, Miss? But Nakoto wears glasses, and has very sharp teeth and enormous eyes; I didn't dare tell him that what I really wanted him to give me was one of the fish. Anyone can understand my point.

It had already gotten dark. We walked for half a block, singing a song off-key that we had perhaps just made up. Gervasio Palmo, by the door to the laundry, looked for the keys in his pocket; it took him a while to find them because he had so many. When he opened the door, we all crowded together and nobody could go in, until Gervasio Palmo called us to order with his thunderous voice. Nakoto made us go over to one side, and turned on the lights in the shop, taking off his glasses. We went into an enormous room I had never seen before. In front of something that looked like a horse's saddle I stopped for a moment to look at the spot where they were going to press Estanislao's suit.

"Shall I take it off?" asked Estanislao.

"No," responded Gervasio, "don't bother. We'll iron it while you have it on."

"And the hump?" asked Estanislao, timidly.

It was the first time that I had ever heard that word, but I figured out what it meant by the context. (You can see I'm working on improving my vocabulary.)

"We'll iron it for you too," answered Gervasio, patting him on the shoulder.

Estanislao lay down on a long table, following instructions from Nakoto, who was getting the irons ready. A smell of ammonia and different acids made me sneeze: I covered my mouth, as you taught me to, Miss, with a handkerchief, but someone called me a pig, which seemed to me like bad manners. What sort of example was that for a child? Nobody was laughing except for Estanislao. All of the men were bumping into things: into the furniture, the doors, the tools, one another. They brought wet rags, flasks, irons. The whole thing, though you may not believe me, resembled a surgical operation. A man fell down on the ground, tripping me so badly that I almost killed myself. Then, at least for me, the fun part was over. I started throwing up. You know I have a healthy stomach and that my classmates at school call me an ostrich because I can swallow anything. I don't know what happened to me. Someone grabbed me, pulled me out of there and took me home.

I didn't see Estanislao Romagan again. Lots of people came to look at the watches and a van from LA PARCA Watch Repair Shop came and took away the last ones, among them my favourite, the one that looked like a wooden house. When I asked my mother where Estanislao was, she didn't want to answer me properly. She told me, as if she were talking to the dog: "He went away," but her eyes were red from weeping over the macrame rug and the knick-knack, and she made me shut up when I mentioned the laundry.

You don't know what I would give for news of Estanislao. When I find out I'll write to you again.

With warmest regards, your favourite student,

N. N.

Mimoso

Mimoso had been on his deathbed for five days. Mercedes fed him milk, fruit juice, and tea with a little spoon. Mercedes called the taxidermist on the phone, giving him the height and length of the dog and inquiring about prices. Embalming him was going to cost a month's salary. She hung up and thought of taking him there right away so that he wouldn't spoil. When she looked in the mirror she saw that her eyes were very swollen from crying; she decided to wait until Mimoso was dead. Sitting next to the kerosene stove, she filled a saucer and started giving the dog spoonfuls of milk again. He no longer opened his mouth and the milk spilt on the floor. At eight o'clock her husband arrived; they cried together, consoling themselves with the thought of the embalming. They imagined the dog standing by the entrance to the room with glass eyes, symbolically guarding the house.

The next morning Mercedes put the dog in a sack. It was perhaps not yet dead. She made a package with burlap and newspaper so as not to attract attention in the bus and took him to the taxidermist's.

In a display case at the house she saw many birds, embalmed monkeys and snakes. She had to wait. The man appeared in shirt sleeves, smoking an Italian cigar. He took the package, saying: "You've

brought the dog. How do you want him?" Mercedes seemed not to
understand. The man took out an album of drawings. "Do you want
him sitting, lying down or standing up? On a wood mount painted
black or white?"

Mercedes looked without saying anything. "Sitting down, with his
little paws crossed."

"With his paws crossed?" the man repeated, as if he didn't like the
idea.

"However you want," Mercedes said, blushing.

It was hot, stiflingly hot. Mercedes took off her coat.

"Let's look at the animal," the man said, opening the package. He
took Mimoso by the back paws, and continued: "He's not so plump as
his owner," laughing loudly. He looked her up and down; she lowered
her eyes and saw her breasts through her tight sweater. "When you see
him he'll be good enough to eat."

Abruptly, Mercedes put on her coat. She squeezed her black kid
gloves in her hands and said, in an attempt to hold back her desire to
slap the man or take the dog away from him: "I want him to have a
wood stand like that one," pointing to one that held a carrier pigeon.

"I can see that madam has good taste," the man mumbled. "And
how do you want the eyes? Glass eyes are a little more expensive."

"Glass eyes," Mercedes answered, biting on her gloves.

"Green, blue, or yellow?"

"Yellow," said Mercedes vehemently. "He had yellow eyes like butterflies."

"Have you ever seen the eyes of butterflies?"

"Like the wings," Mercedes protested, "like the wings of butterflies."

"That's more like it! You have to pay in advance," the man said.

"I know," Mercedes answered, "you told me on the phone." She
opened her wallet and took out the bills; she counted them and left
them on the table. The man gave her a receipt. "When will he be ready
for me to pick him up?" she asked, putting away the receipt in her
wallet.

"There's no need for that. I'll bring him to your house on the twentieth of next month."

"I'll come pick him up with my husband," Mercedes answered,
rushing suddenly out of the house.

Mercedes's friends found out that the dog had died and wanted to know what they had done with the body. Mercedes told them that they had had it embalmed, and nobody believed her. Many people laughed. She decided it was better to say they had dumped it some-where. Holding her knitting, she sat like Penelope, knitting, awaiting the arrival of the embalmed dog. But the dog didn't come. Mercedes was still crying and drying her tears with a flowered handkerchief.

On the appointed day Mercedes got a phone call: the dog had been embalmed, and all they had to do was go and get him. The man couldn't deliver so far away. Mercedes and her husband went to fetch the dog in a taxi.

"What we have had to spend on this dog," Mercedes's husband said in the cab, watching the increasing numbers.

"A child would not have cost more," said Mercedes, taking a hand-kerchief out of her pocket and drying her tears.

"Well, that's enough; you've already cried plenty."

At the taxidermist's they had to wait. Mercedes did not talk, but her husband looked at her attentively.

"Won't people say you're crazy?" her husband inquired with a smile.

"So much the worse for them," responded Mercedes vehemently. "They have no heart, and life is very sad for those without hearts. Nobody loves them."

"I think so too, sweetheart."

The taxidermist brought the dog almost too promptly. There was Mimoso, mounted on a piece of dark, varnished wood, half-sitting, with glass eyes and a varnished mouth. He had never looked in better health. He was fat, well-brushed, and shiny; the only thing he couldn't do was talk. Mercedes caressed him with trembling hands; tears burst from her eyes and fell on the dog's head.

"Don't get him wet," said the taxidermist. "And wash your hands."

"He looks as if he could talk," said Mercedes's husband. "How do you accomplish such miracles?"

"With poison, sir. I do the whole job with poison, putting on gloves and glasses, otherwise I would poison myself. It's my own system. There are no children in your house?"

"No."

"Will he be a danger to us?" asked Mercedes.

"Only if you eat him."

"We have to wrap him up," said Mercedes, after wiping her tears.

The taxidermist wrapped the embalmed animal in newspaper and gave Mercedes's husband the package. They went out joyfully. On the way they talked about where they would put Mimoso. They chose the foyer of the house, next to the telephone table, where Mimoso would wait for them when they went out.

At home, after examining the taxidermist's work, they put the dog in the place they had chosen. Mercedes sat next to him to look at him: this dead dog would keep her company as the same dog had kept her company when he was alive, would defend her from thieves and from society. She caressed the head with her fingertips and, at a moment when she believed that her husband was not watching, she gave him a furtive kiss.

"What will your friends say when they see this?" her husband inquired. "What will the bookseller at Merluchi's say?"

"When he comes to dinner I will put Mimoso away in the dresser or say he's a present from the lady on the third floor."

"You'll have to tell the lady that."

"I shall," said Mercedes.

That night they drank a very special wine and went to bed later than usual.

The lady on the third floor smiled when Mercedes made her request. She understood the perversity of a world in which a woman could not have her dog embalmed without people thinking she was crazy.

Mercedes was happier with the embalmed dog than with the live one; she didn't have to feed him, didn't have to take him outside, didn't have to bathe him, and he didn't mess up the house or chew the rug. But happiness never lasts. Evil talk arrived in the form of an anonymous letter. An obscene drawing illustrated the words. Mercedes's husband shook with indignation: the fire in the oven was cooler than his heart. He took the dog on his knee, broke him in various pieces as if he were a dry branch, and threw him in the open oven.

"Whether or not what they say is true doesn't matter, what matters is that they're saying it."

"You'll not keep me from dreaming about him," Mercedes cried, going to bed with her clothes on. "I know who the perverse man is who sends these anonymous letters. It's that vendor of pornography.

He'll never set foot in this house again."

"You'll have to receive him. He's coming to dinner tonight."

"Tonight?" said Mercedes. She jumped out of bed and ran to the kitchen to make dinner, a smile on her lips. She put the dog next to the steak in the oven.

She made dinner earlier than usual.

"We're having meat cooked in the hide," Mercedes announced.

At the door, even before saying hello, the guest rubbed his hands when he smelled what was in the oven. Later, when he was being served, he said: "These animals look as if they were embalmed," looking with wonder at the dog's eyes.

"In China," Mercedes said, "I've been told they eat dogs. Is that true or is it a shaggy dog story?"

"I don't know. In any case, I wouldn't eat them for anything in the world."

"You should never say 'dog eat dog,'" responded Mercedes with a charming smile.

The guest was amazed that Mercedes could talk so frankly about dogs.

"We'll have to call the barber," said the guest, seeing some hairs in his meat cooked in the hide, and, with a hearty, contagious laugh, he asked: "Do you eat meat cooked in the hide with a sauce?"

"It's something new," Mercedes answered.

The guest served himself from the bowl, sucked on a piece of meat covered with sauce, chewed on it, and fell down dead.

"Mimoso still defends me," said Mercedes, picking up the plates and drying her tears, for she was laughing and crying at the same time.

The Velvet Dress

Sweating, mopping our brows with handkerchiefs that we moistened in the Recoleta fountain, we came to that house on Ayacucho Street, the one with a garden. How funny!

We went up in the elevator to the fifth floor. I was in a foul mood, because I didn't want to go out: my dress was dirty and I had planned to spend the afternoon washing and ironing my bedspread. We rang the bell: the door opened and we, Casilda and I, went into the house, with the package. Casilda is a dressmaker. We live in Burzaco and our trips into the capital make her ill, especially when we have to go to the northern part of the city, which is so out of the way. Casilda asked the servant for a glass of water right away to take the aspirin she had in her purse. The aspirin fell on the floor along with the glass and the purse. How funny!

We went up a carpeted staircase (smelling of mothballs), preceded by the servant, who showed us into the bedroom of Mrs Cornelia Catalpina, whose very name was torture for me to remember. The bedroom was all red, with white drapes and mirrors in golden frames. We waited for a century or so for a lady to come from the next room, where we could hear her gargling and arguing with various voices. Her perfume entered; then, a few moments later, she herself entered

43

with a different perfume. She greeted us with a complaint: "How
lucky you are to live in the outskirts of Buenos Aires! At least there's no
soot there. There may be rabid dogs and garbage dumps . . . Look at
my bedspread. Do you think it's supposed to be grey? No. It's white. A
snowflake." She took me by the chin and added: "You don't have to
worry about things like that. What a joy to be young! You're eight,
aren't you?" Then, addressing Casilda, she added: "Why don't you put
a stone on her head so she won't grow up? We're young only as long as
our children are."

Everyone thought my friend Casilda was my mother. How funny!

"Ma'am, do you want to try it on?" Casilda asked, opening the
package which was all pinned together. She told me: "Take the pins
from my wallet."

"Trying things on! That's torture for me! If someone could try on
my dresses for me, how happy I would be! It's so tiring."

The lady undressed and Casilda tried to help her put on the velvet
dress.

"When is the trip supposed to be, ma'am? " she asked to distract her.

The lady couldn't answer. The dress was stuck on her shoulders:
something kept it from going past her neck. How funny!

"Velvet is very sticky, ma'am, and it's hot today. Let's put on a little
talcum powder."

"Take it off, I'm suffocating," the lady cried out.

Casilda took the dress and the lady sat down in an armchair, about
to faint.

"When is the trip supposed to be, ma'am?" Casilda asked again to
distract her.

"I'm leaving any day now. Today, thanks to airplanes, you can leave
whenever you feel like it. The dress will have to be ready. To think that
there it's snowing. Everything is white, clean and shiny."

"You're going to Paris?"

"I'm also going to Italy."

"Won't you try on the dress again, ma'am? We'll be finished in a moment."

The lady nodded with a sigh.

"Raise both your arms so we can first put on the two sleeves,"
Casilda said, taking the dress and helping her put it on once again.

For a few seconds Casilda tried unsuccessfully to pull the skirt of the dress down over the lady's hips. I helped as best as I could. She finally managed to put on the dress. For a few moments the lady rested, exhausted, in the armchair; then she stood up to look at herself in the mirror. The dress was beautiful and complicated! A dragon embroidered with black sequins was shining on the left side of the gown. Casilda knelt down, looking in the mirror, and adjusted the hem. Then she stood up and began putting pins in the folds of the gown, on the neck and sleeves. I touched the velvet: it was rough when you rubbed it one way and smooth when you rubbed it the other. The plush set my teeth on edge. The pins fell on the wood floor, and I picked them up religiously, one by one. How funny!

"What a dress! I don't think there's such a beautiful pattern in all of Buenos Aires," said Casilda, letting a pin drop from her lips. "Don't you like it, ma'am?"

"Very much. Velvet is my favourite material. Fabric is like flowers: one has one's favourites. I think that velvet is like spikenard."

"Do you like spikenard? It's so sad," Casilda protested.

"Spikenard is my favourite flower, yet it's harmful to me. When I smell it I get sick. Velvet sets my teeth on edge, gives me goose-pimples, the same as linen gloves used to when I was a girl, and yet for me there's no other fabric like it in the world. To feel its softness with my hand attracts me even though at times it repels me. What woman is better dressed than one who wears black velvet? She doesn't need a lace collar, nor a string of pearls; everything else is unnecessary. Velvet is sufficient by itself. It's sumptuous and sober."

When she had finished talking, the lady was breathing with difficulty. The dragon also. Casilda took a newspaper from the table and fanned her, but the lady made her stop, saying that fresh air did her no good. How funny!

In the street I heard the cries of some street vendors. What were they selling? Fruit, ice cream perhaps? The whistle of the knife sharpener and the ringing bell of the ice cream vendor also ran up and down the street. I didn't run to the window to see, as I had on other occasions. I didn't tire of watching the fittings of the dress with the sequin dragon. The lady stood up again and, staggering slightly, went over to the mirror. The sequin dragon also staggered. The dress was now almost perfect, except for an almost imperceptible tuck under the arms. Casilda once more took the pins and plunged them perilously into the wrinkles that bulged out of the unearthly fabric.

"When you grow up," the lady told me, "you'd like to have a velvet dress, wouldn't you?"

"Yes," I answered, and I felt the velvet of that dress strangling my neck with its gloved hands. How funny!

"Now you'll help me off with it," the lady said.

Casilda tried to help her take it off, holding the hem in both hands. She pulled on it unsuccessfully for a few seconds, then put it back on the way it was before.

"I'll have to sleep in it," the lady said, standing in front of the mirror, looking at her pale face and the dragon trembling with each beat of her heart. "Velvet is marvellous but heavy," she said, wiping her forehead with her hand. "It's a prison. How to escape? They should make dresses of fabric as immaterial as air, light or water."

"I recommended raw silk to you," Casilda protested.

The lady fell to the floor, and the dragon writhed. Casilda leaned over the body until the dragon lay still. I again caressed the velvet, which seemed like a live animal. Casilda said sadly: "She's dead. I had so much trouble making this dress! It cost me so very, very much!"

How funny!

The Objects

For her twentieth birthday someone gave Camila Ersky a golden bracelet with a rose of rubies. It was a family heirloom. She liked the bracelet and wore it only on certain occasions when she was going to some gathering or to the theatre for opening night. Nonetheless, when she lost it she did not share the pain of her loss with the rest of the family. In her view, objects could not be replaced whatever their value; she appreciated only people, the canaries who adorned her house, and the dogs. In the course of her life, I think she wept only at the loss of a silver chain, with a medal of the Virgin of Lujan set in gold, a present from one of her boyfriends. The idea of losing things, those things we lose as if by fate, did not trouble her as much as it did the rest of the family or her friends, who were a vain lot. Without tears she had seen her childhood home stripped, once by fire, once by a poverty as zealous as fire: stripped of its most beloved furnishings (paintings, tables, commodes, screens, vases, bronze statues, fans, marble cherubs, porcelain dancers, bottles of perfume in the shape of radishes, whole cases of miniatures with curls and beards), horrible sometimes but valuable. I suspect that her complacency was not a sign of indifference, and that she had an anxious foreboding that these objects would someday rob her of something more precious than her

childhood. Perhaps she cared for them more than did those others
who wept over their loss. Sometimes she saw these objects. They came
to visit her like people, in processions, especially at night, when she
was about to fall asleep, when she was travelling by train or by car, or
even when she was going through her daily routine on her way to
work. Often they bothered her like insects: she wanted to scare them
off, to think of other things. Often, from a lack of imagination, she
described them to her children, in the stories she told them to entertain them as they ate. She did not add to the objects' glow or beauty or
mystery: that was not necessary.

One afternoon, returning from some errands, she crossed a square
and stopped to rest on a bench. Why think of Buenos Aires? There are
other cities with squares. The light of the setting sun bathed the branches, the streets, the houses around her: the light that sometimes
increases the sagacity of joy. She contemplated the sky for quite a
while, stroking her stained kid gloves; then, attracted by something
shiny on the ground, she looked down and after a few moments saw
the bracelet she had lost more than fifteen years before. With the emotion that saints must feel when they work their first miracle, she
picked the object up. Night fell before she decided to put the bracelet
on her left wrist as she had long ago.

When she got home, after looking at her wrist to make sure that the
bracelet had not vanished, she told the news to her children, who did
not interrupt their games, and to her husband, who looked at her
skeptically, never stopping his reading of the paper. For days, despite
her children's indifference and her husband's suspicions, she woke up
with the joy of having found the bracelet. The only people who would
have been properly surprised were all dead.

She began to remember with greater precision the objects that had
peopled her life; she remembered them with nostalgia, with an
unknown anxiety. Like an inventory, in reverse chronological order,
her memory was filled with a crystal dove with broken wings and beak;
a candy box in the shape of a piano; a bronze statue that held up a
lantern with little light bulbs; the bronze clock; the marble cushion
with bluish streaks and tassels; the opera glasses with a mother-of-
pearl handle; the inscribed cup; and the ivory monkeys with little
baskets full of baby monkeys.

In a way that seemed completely normal to her and is completely incredible to us, she slowly recovered the objects that had dwelled in her memory for so long.

At the same time she noticed that the happiness she had felt at first was turning into a feeling of discomfort, of fear, of worry.

She hardly looked at the things around her for fear of discovering a lost treasure.

While Camila was troubled and tried to think of other things, the objects appeared, in the market, at stores, in hotels, anywhere at all, everything from the bronze statue with the torch that used to light up the entrance to the house, to the jewelled heart crossed by an arrow. The gypsy doll and the kaleidoscope were the last ones. Where did she find those toys, belonging to her childhood? I am ashamed to say, because you, my readers, will think that I seek only to surprise you and not to tell the truth. You will think that the toys were others, similar to the old ones, not the very same, that of course there is not only one gypsy doll in the whole world, not only one kaleidoscope. But fate had it that the doll's arm was tattooed with a butterfly in India ink and that, engraved on the copper tube, the kaleidoscope had the name of Camila Ersky.

If it were not so pathetic, this story would be tedious. If it does not seem pathetic to you, my readers, at least it's short, and telling it will give me practise. In the dressing rooms of the theatres that Camila often attended, she found the toys that belonged, by a long series of coincidences, to the daughter of a dancer; the girl insisted on trading them for a mechanical bear and a plastic circus. She came home with the old toys wrapped in newspaper. Several times, on the way home, she wanted to put the package down at the bottom of a staircase or on the threshold of some door.

Nobody was home. She opened the windows wide, taking a deep breath of the evening air. Then she saw the objects lined up against the wall of her room, just as she had dreamed she would see them. She knelt down to caress them. She lost track of day and night. She saw that the objects had faces, those horrible faces they assume when we have stared at them too long.

Through a long series of joys, Camila Ersky had finally entered hell.

The Bed

They loved each other, but jealousy (whether jealousy of the past or the future), a common feeling of envy, and a common lack of confidence were gnawing away at them. Sometimes, in a bed, they forgot these unfortunate feelings, and thanks to it they survived. I will tell of one of these instances, the last one.

The bed was fluffy and wide and was covered with a pink spread. The centre of the headboard, which was of iron, showed a landscape with trees and ships. The setting sun was illuminating a cloud shaped like a flame. When they embraced, the one lucky enough to be lying face up kissing the other mouth, attracted by the unusual radiance that filled that cloud, could look at it through the fringes of a lamp decorated with red and green tulips.

They lingered longer than usual in the bed. The sounds from the street grew louder and then died down as darkness fell. You might have thought the bed was sailing on a sea outside time and space, searching for happiness or for some convincing likeness of it. But there are reckless lovers. Their clothes, which they had taken off, were nearby, within reach. The empty sleeves of a shirt hung from the bed, and a light-blue piece of paper had fallen out of one of the pockets. Someone picked up the paper. I don't know what that sky-blue paper had on it, but I know that it produced commotion, investigations, irrepressible hatred, arguments, reconciliations, new arguments.

Dawn was peeking in the windows.

"I smell a fire. Last night I dreamt of fire," she said, in a moment of horror, facing his anger, trying to distract him.

"Your sense of smell is fooling you," he said.

"We're on the ninth floor," she added, trying to look scared. "I'm afraid."

"Don't change the subject."

"I'm not changing the subject. The fire makes sounds like falling water, can't you hear it?"

"Your ears are fooling you."

The room was brightly lit and hot. It was a bonfire.

"If we embraced, only our backs would burn up."

"We'll burn up completely," he said, looking at the fire with furious eyes.

The Perfect Crime

Gilberta Pax wanted to live in peace. When I fell in love with her I believed the opposite; I offered her everything a man in my position can offer a woman to persuade her to come live with me, since we could not marry. For one or two years we met in uncomfortable, expensive places. First in cars, then in cafes, then in seedy movie theatres, then in rather dirty hotels. Once, when I didn't ask but rather demanded that she live with me, she answered: "I can't."

"Why not?" I asked. "Because of your husband?"

"Because of the cook," she whispered, and she went running out.

Angrily, the next day I asked for an explanation. She gave it to me.

You don't know my house; it's like a hotel [she said]. Five people live there with us; besides my husband, there's my uncle, one of his sisters and his two children. They want everything to be perfect, especially the food; but Tomas Mangorsino, the cook—who's been with us for eight years—made fun of us. Although the appearance of each dish was rather pleasing, each day he would cook worse. My hair smelling of grease, for I forgot to cover it with a kerchief, I would spend the morning asking him to cook as well as he did in his prime. Mangorsino looked at me with some compassion, but never obeyed me. One morning when I visited him in a pink bathrobe and a green plastic cap, the kind you could wear to a dance, he stared at me so insistently that I asked him: "What's wrong, Mangorsino?"

"What's wrong? This morning my lady is so beautiful that I hardly recognize her."

That was when I had the idea of sacrificing myself to my duty as a housewife by seducing him. As if he had guessed my intention, he changed his behaviour, but only toward me. He sent meringue puffs, in shapes that suggested his love, in portions large enough for only one person. When he spoke to me, I could sense repressed tenderness in the tone of his voice.

"Make some noodles with a very light dough."

"I'll knead it very well," he would say, looking me in the eye.

Or else: "And the turnover I like?"

"I'll brown it. I know you'll like it."

"And what are you going to make for tea?"

"Meringue kisses."

He said all of that while eating me with his wolf's eyes.

I acceded to his demands, but things didn't change much. He would send me a dish, forbidding me to eat what was in it, which was the portion for the others, cheaper and not as fresh. The servant would whisper to me, while setting the plate on the table in front of me: "This is for my lady, whose digestion is a bit delicate."

The situation became horribly prolonged. While the rest of the family writhed from stomachache, I ate delicious pastries which, if they had not endangered my slim figure, would have delighted me.

"My husband wants to eat mushrooms (I hate them, and wouldn't even eat them in a pastry) and my children want turkey," I told him one day.

He almost strangled me.

"They are very expensive," he answered.

At the same time our relationship began to be troubled by misunderstandings. When he sharpens the knives, he stares intently at my neck. I am afraid of him, why deny it? When he twists a dishrag I know he is twisting my neck; when he slices meat, he is slicing me. At night I can't sleep. I'm a slave of his fancies.

"Don't worry," I told Gilberta. "Where does he buy meat and

vegetables?"

"I have the address in my address book," she told me. "1000 Junin Street. Do you plan to kill him?"

"Something better than that," I answered.

It was the middle of the winter and I went to the country to gather mushrooms. I brought them home in a sack. I asked Gilberta for a photograph of Tomas Mangorsino.

"What do you want it for?" she asked.

"I also have my ideas," I answered. She brought me the picture.

To carry out my plan, I needed to know what Mangorsino was like. After finding out what time he went to the market, I stationed myself at a corner I knew he passed at seven every morning. A man went by in an impeccable grey suit and a brown scarf. I consulted the photograph: it was Mangorsino.

"Mushrooms, extremely cheap," I cried, with a peddler's voice, "very fresh."

Mangorsino stopped, looked at my gloves. I didn't want to leave fingerprints, just in case.

"How much?"

"Five pesos," I said, speaking like a foreigner.

"Give them to me," he said, taking money from a bottomless pocket.

The next day, in the afternoon paper, I read the news. A whole family had died, poisoned by mushrooms bought in the street by the cook, Mangorsino. The only survivor is Mrs Gilberta Pax.

I went to the house, where Gilberta was waiting for me. I told her nothing of what I had done. Such a complicated, subtle crime should not be confided to anyone, not even to the person you love most in the world, not even to your pillow.

She told me that her family felt indignant as they were dying and didn't lose their senses: when they felt the first symptoms of the poison they ran, forks in hand, into the kitchen, where they forced Mangorsino also to eat the poisonous mushrooms, which caused the poor man's death. My crime was a crime of passion and, what is more unusual, a perfect one.

Azabache

I am Argentine. I joined the crew of a ship. In Marseille I found a doctor to sign a document certifying that I was crazy. It was easy for him
to do because he may have been crazy himself. That way I was able to
leave the ship, but they shut me up in an insane asylum and now I have
no hope that anyone will ever be able to get me out.

This is my story: to escape from my country I joined a ship's crew,
and to escape from the ship I got shut up in an insane asylum. When
I fled from my country and when I fled from the ship I thought I was
fleeing from my memories, but every day I relive the story of my love,
which is my prison. They say that I fell in love with Aurelia because of
my hatred of elegant women, but that's not true. I loved her as I never
loved any other woman in my life. Aurelia was a servant; she barely
knew how to read or write. Her eyes were black, her hair black and
straight like a horse's mane. As soon as she finished washing the dishes
or the floors she would take a pencil and paper and go to a corner to
draw horses. That was all she knew how to draw: horses galloping,
jumping, sitting, lying down. Sometimes they were roan, other times
chestnut, red, bay, black, bluish, white. Sometimes she drew them with
chalk, when she could find chalk; other times with coloured pencils,
when someone gave her some; other times with ink or paint. They all

had names: her favourite was Azabache, because he was jet-black and skittish.

When she brought me my breakfast in the morning, I would hear her laughter, which sounded like neighing, for a few moments before she came into my bedroom, kicking nervously against the door. I was unable to educate her, in fact refused to educate her. I fell in love with her.

I had to leave my parents' house and went to live with her in Chascomus, on the outskirts of town. It was the proliferating walls of a city, I thought, that cause our unhappiness. With joy I sold all of my things, my car and my furniture, to be able to rent the tiny farm where I could live simply, enchanted by that impossible love. At auction I bought some cows and the herd of horses I needed to work the land.

At first I was happy. What did it matter not having indoor plumbing or electric light or a refrigerator or clean sheets! Love replaced all of that. Aurelia had bewitched me. What did it matter that the soles of her feet were rough, that her hands were always red, and that her manners were not the finest: I was her slave!

She liked eating sugar. I would put sugar cubes in the palm of my hand, and she would eat them. She liked me to stroke her on the head: I would caress her for hours on end.

Sometimes I would look for her all day long without finding her anywhere. How could she find a hiding place on that piece of land, which was completely flat and treeless? She would come back barefoot, with her hair so tangled that no comb could smooth it. I warned her that along the coast, not very far away, there were swamps full of crabs.

Sometimes I'd find her talking to the horses. She, who was so quiet, would speak incessantly with them. They loved her and would gather around her. Her favourite was named Azabache.

Some people called me a degenerate; others, but there were not so many of them, felt sorry for me. They sold me bad meat, and at the store they tried to charge me twice for the same bills, thinking me absent-minded. Living in that hostile solitude was bad for me.

I married Aurelia so that they would sell me better-quality meat at the butcher shop; that is what my enemies said, but I can assure them that I did it to live in a respectable fashion. Aurelia amused herself kissing the noses of the horses; she would braid her hair to the horses' manes. These games showed her youth and the tenderness of her heart. She was mine, as that horrible elegant woman, with painted nails, with whom I had fallen in love years before, had never been mine.

One afternoon I found Aurelia speaking to a tramp about horses. I didn't understand anything they were saying. I took Aurelia by the arm and dragged her home, without saying a word. That day she cooked unwillingly and broke the door by kicking it too hard. I locked her up inside and told her I was punishing her for speaking with strangers. She seemed not to understand me. She slept until I let her out.

So that she wouldn't venture far from the house again I told her how people and animals had died after falling in the swamps, devoured by the crabs. She didn't listen to me. I took her by the arm and shouted in her ear. She stood up and left the house with head high, walking toward the coast.

"Where are you going?" I asked her.

She kept on walking without speaking to me. I held her by the dress, struggling with her until it tore. I knocked her down, hurting her in my desperation. She stood up and kept on walking. I followed her. When we got near the river, I asked her not to go on because there were the swamps, with foul-smelling mud. She kept on walking. She took a narrow path through the swamps. I followed her. Our feet sank in the mud and we heard the cry of countless birds. No trees were to be seen, and reeds filled the horizon. We reached a place where the trail turned; there we saw Azabache, the black horse, sunk in the swamp up to his belly. Aurelia stopped for a moment without showing surprise. Quickly, in a single leap, she jumped in the swamp and began sinking. While she was trying to get nearer the horse, I tried to reach her and save her. I lay down in the swamp, slipping along like a reptile. I took her by the arm and began to sink in with her. For a few moments I thought I was going to die. I looked her in the eye and saw that strange light that appears in the eyes of the dying: I saw the horse reflected in them. I released her arm. Until dawn, slipping along like a worm on the disgusting surface of the swamp, I waited for the end (which was endless for me) of Aurelia and Azabache, both of whom finally sank.

Friends

Many misfortunes happened in our village. A flood cut us off from the centre of town. I remember that for two months we could not go to school or to the drugstore. The currents of the river, which had overflowed its banks, made some of the walls of the school fall down. The next year an epidemic of typhoid fever killed my aunt, who was a very devout but severe woman, as well as the teacher and the parish priest, so respected by my parents. In three weeks thirty people died. Nearly the whole town was in mourning; the cemetery looked like a flower show, and the streets sounded like a bell-ringing contest.

My friend Cornelio lived on the third floor of our house. We were seven years old. We were like brothers because our families were so close. We shared games, parents, aunts, meals. We went to school together. Cornelio learned any lesson easily, but didn't like studying. I learned with difficulty, but liked studying. Cornelio hated the teacher; I liked her.

"He'll be made a saint," Aunt Fermina said sadly.

"It's just a phase he's going through," said Aunt Claudia, who looked like an ostrich. "Don't worry."

As an ostrich shakes its wings, she shook her shoulders when she spoke.

"What's wrong with being a saint?" my mother asked all of a sudden.

"If it were your son, you wouldn't much like it," Cornelio's mother answered.

"Why not? Isn't it good to be on good terms with God?"

"The hair shirt, the fasting, the retreats," Cornelio's mother said slowly, with terror and at the same time with a kind of pleasure.

"Do you prefer drinking or women or politics? Are you afraid that they'll steal your son from you? God or the world will take him from you."

"God? That's a more serious matter."

Our mothers smiled sadly, as if they had come to an agreement. I listened in silence. I had seen Cornelio in his white smock, a missal in hand, kneeling by the window, praying, at the strangest times. When I came into his room, he pretended, blushing all the while, to be study-ing grammar or the history textbook, quickly hiding the missal under his chair or in a drawer so that I wouldn't see it. I asked myself, why is he ashamed of his piety? Does he think prayer is something like play-ing with dolls? He never confided in me or spoke about religious mat-ters. Despite our youth, we acted like men and spoke frankly of girlfriends, sex and marriage. That contradicted Cornelio's withdrawn, mystical attitude.

"When I pray to be granted a favour, it is granted," he told me one day, singing proudly to himself.

I told my aunts what he had said, and they commented on it for a long time. They attributed Cornelio's devotion to the strong impres-sions made on him by the catastrophes that had afflicted our town. When a boy our age had seen so many deaths in such a short time, it had to make some impression on his soul. If these events had not affected my own character, it was because I was by nature insensitive and a bit perverse. Cornelio's mysticism had begun before the flood and the epidemic; hence, it was absurd to attribute it to those cir-cumstances. I hinted darkly at the mistake all the adults were making, but as usual kept quiet and accepted what they said. So I embraced my role as a perverse child, unlike Cornelio, who was the personification of sensitivity and goodness. I never failed to feel jealous and surprised by the involuntary guilt of my inferiority. Often, shut up in my room, I'd cry for my sins, asking God to grant me the favour of making me more like my friend once again.

The control Cornelio had over me was great: never did I want to disagree with him, or displease or hurt him, but he forced me to disagree with him, displease him, hurt him.

One day he got annoyed because I had taken his penknife. I had to play tricks like that on him so he would not despise me. Another day I took his tool box; he hit and scratched me.

"If you ever touch any of my other things, I'll pray for your death," he said. I laughed. "You don't believe me? Wasn't there a flood and an epidemic a while ago? Do you think it was by chance?"

"The flood?" I asked.

"I caused it. It was my doing."

He may not have said these exact words, but he spoke like a man and his words were deliberate.

"Why?"

"In order not to have to go to school. Why else? What else could one pray for?"

"And the epidemic?" I murmured, holding my breath.

"That too. That was even less trouble."

"Why?"

"So the teacher and my aunt would die. I can make you die too, if I feel like it."

I laughed, because I knew he would despise me if I didn't. In the mirror of the wardrobe, across from us, I saw myself frowning. I froze with fear, and as soon as I could went running to my aunts to recount to them my conversation with my friend. My aunts laughed at my distress.

"It's just a joke," they said. "The boy's a saint."

But Rita, my cousin, who looked like an old woman and always listened in on other people's conversations, said: "He's not a saint. He doesn't even pray to God. He has a pact with the devil. Haven't you seen his missal? The cover is the same as every other missal but the inside is different. Nothing that is printed on those horrible pages makes sense. Do you want to see it? Bring the book," she ordered me. "It's in the drawer of the bureau, wrapped in a handkerchief."

I hesitated. How could I betray Cornelio? Secrets are sacred, but finally weakness won out. I went to Cornelio's room and, trembling, took out the missal, which was wrapped in a handkerchief. My aunt

Claudia untied the corners of the handkerchief and took out the book. Pages were pasted on top of the original pages. I saw the incomprehensible signs and devilish drawings that Rita had described.

"What are we to do?" my aunts said.

Cornelio's mother gave me back the book and ordered me: "You can put it back where you found it," and addressing Rita, "You deserve to be sued for slander. If only we were in England!"

My aunts hissed like owls that have been disturbed.

"The boy's a saint. He may have his own language to speak to God," my mother declared, staring severely at Rita, who was choking on a mint.

"And if he makes me die?"

All of the women laughed, even Rita, who a few moments before had asserted that there was a pact between Cornelio and the devil.

Did adults mean anything serious when they spoke? Who could believe me or take me seriously? Rita had made fun of me. So then, to prove the veracity of my words, I went up to Cornelio's room and, instead of putting the missal back in the drawer, I put it in my pocket and took the object that he most treasured: a plastic watch with moving hands.

I remember it was late and the whole family had gathered for dinner. As it was summertime, after dinner I went out in the garden with my aunt. No doubt Cornelio had not yet gone into his room or noticed that anything was missing.

What power did Cornelio have that made his prayers be answered? What sort of death would he demand for me? Fire, water, blood? All of these words crossed my mind until I heard steps in the corridor and in his room. I couldn't tell the muffled sound of the steps from that of my heart. I was about to flee, to bury the watch and the missal in the garden, but I knew I couldn't fool Cornelio because he was in league with some power greater than our own. I heard him call me: his cry was a roar, tearing my name apart. I went up the stairs to his room. I stopped for a moment on the landing, observing his movements through the half-open door; then I went up the creaky, broken ladder to the attic. Cornelio questioned me from the other landing and I, instead of answering him, threw the book and the watch at his head. He didn't say anything. He picked them up. He knelt down and eagerly read the pages. For the first time Cornelio was not ashamed to be seen praying. The step where I was standing creaked and then suddenly gave way: when I fell I banged my head against the iron bars of the balustrade.

When I came to, the whole family was gathered around me; Cornelio sat still in a corner of the room with his arms crossed.

I had no doubt I was going to die, as I could see the faces peering over my own as if looking down a well.

"Why don't you ask God to save your little friend? Didn't you say that God grants you everything you ask for?" my aunt Fermina dared to whisper.

Cornelio prostrated himself on the floor like a Muslim. He banged his head against the floor and answered with the voice of a spoiled child: "I can only bring sickness or death."

My mother looked at him with horror and knelt down next to him, tugging on his hair as if he were a dog, and saying: "Try, my child. You don't lose anything by praying. God will have to hear you."

For days I floated in a pink-and-blue limbo, between life and death. The voices were farther away. I could not recognize the faces: they were floating at the bottom of the water. When I recovered, two months later, they gave Cornelio credit for my good luck: according to my aunts and our mothers, he had saved me. Once again I heard them sing the praises of Cornelio's saintliness. They no longer remembered the tears they had shed for me, nor the fondness that the gravity of my illness had inspired in them. Once again I found myself the insensitive and somewhat perverse child, so inferior to my friend.

Through my aunts, the seamstress, and some friends of the household, contradictory details about what had happened reached the people in town. There were comments on Cornelio's mystical tendencies. Some people held that my friend was a saint, others that he was a sorcerer and that it was better not to come to our house, because of his maledictions. When my aunt Claudia got married, nobody came to the reception.

Was Cornelio a sorcerer or a saint? Night after night, turning my pillow over in search of a cool place to rest my feverish head, I thought of Cornelio's saintliness—or was it witchcraft? Had even Rita forgotten her suspicions?

One day we went fishing at the Arroyo del Sauce. We took along a picnic basket of food, to spend the day there. Our neighbour Andres, who loved fishing, was already standing on the bank with his rod ready. A dog came up and walked around playing cute tricks, as lost dogs are wont to do. Andres said he would take it home; Cornelio said he was going to; they started arguing about that. They started punching one another and Cornelio fell down, beaten. Andres, conceited as could be, fixed his rod, took the dog in his arms, and left. Lying on the ground, Cornelio began reciting his curses: the noise his lips made was like that of a liquid about to come to a boil. Andres had walked only about twenty paces when he fell down: foam came from his mouth. The dog, now free, ran toward us. We later found out that Andres had had an epileptic seizure.

When Cornelio and I walked down the street, people whispered: they knew he was a sorcerer, not the saint our family thought. One Good Friday the children wouldn't let us go into the church: they threw stones at us.

What could I do to punish Cornelio? Would my death achieve something, serve as evidence of my truthfulness and his perversity? For a moment I imagined his life ruined forevermore, pursued by my memory, as was Cain by Abel. I sought out some means of infuriating him. I had to make his curses fall on me once again. I lamented that death would prevent me from bearing witness to his remorse, when his will would be done. Would remorse hold him back from repeating those accursed prayers?

We were on the banks of the Arroyo del Sauce. We watched a kingfisher plunging into the water over and over with dizzying speed. Each of us had a slingshot. We aimed: Cornelio at the kingfisher, I in the air, so that my shot would go astray. Cornelio, who was a good shot, hit the bird on the head, and it fell down, wounded. We jumped in the water to catch it. Then, on shore, an argument began about who had killed the kingfisher. I firmly insisted that the catch was mine.

There was a very deep place in the stream, where we couldn't stand. I knew where it was, because it looked like a sort of eddy. My father had pointed it out to me. I picked up the bird and ran along the bank until I reached the place where I could see the mysterious stirring of the water. Andres was nearby, fishing as always. I stopped and threw the kingfisher into the whirlpool. Cornelio, who was chasing after me, threw himself down on his knees. I heard the terrifying murmur on his lips; he was repeating my name. A cold sweat bathed the back of my neck, my arms, my hair. The fields, the trees, the ravines, the stream, Andres, everything started shaking, spinning around. I saw Death with his scythe. Then I heard Cornelio utter his own name. Such was my surprise that I did not hear him jump in the water; he did not try to reach the bird; he struggled in the water, going under, since he did not know how to swim. Andres, calm as could be, shouted at him with a bitter voice, like a parrot: "Idiot. What good is your sorcery to you now?"

I understood, years later, that at the last moment Cornelio changed the content of his last prayer: to save me, instead of asking for my death, which had perhaps already been granted, he asked for his own death.

The House of Sugar

Superstitions kept Cristina from living. A coin with a blurry face, a spot of ink, the moon seen through two panes of glass, the initials of her name carved by chance on the trunk of a cedar: all these would make her mad with fear. The day we met she was wearing a green dress; she kept wearing it until it fell apart, since she said it brought her luck and that as soon as she wore another, a blue one which fit her better, we would no longer see each other. I tried to combat these absurd manias. I made her take note that she had a broken mirror in her room, yet she insisted on keeping it, no matter how I insisted that it was better to throw broken mirrors into water some moonlit night to get rid of the bad luck. She was never afraid if the light in the house went out all of a sudden; despite the fact that it was a definite omen of death, she would light any number of candles without thinking twice. She always left her hat on the bed, a mistake nobody else made. Her fears were more individual. She inflicted real privations on herself; for instance, she could not eat strawberries in the summertime, or hear certain pieces of music, or adorn her house with goldfish, which she liked so much. There were certain streets we could not cross, certain persons we could not see, certain movie theatres we could not frequent. At the beginning of our relationship, these superstitions seemed charming to me, but later they began to annoy and even seriously worry me. When we got engaged we had to look for a brand-new apartment because according to her beliefs, the fate of the previous occupants would influence her life. (She at no point mentioned my life, as if the danger threatened only hers and our lives were not joined by love.) We visited all of the neighbourhoods in the city; we went even to the most distant suburbs in search of an apartment where no one had ever lived, but they had all been rented or sold. Finally I found a little house on Montes de Oca Street that looked like it was made of sugar. Its whiteness gleamed with extraordinary brilliance. It had a phone and a tiny garden in front. I thought that house was newly built, but found out that a family had occupied it in 1930 and that later, in order to rent it, the owner had remodelled it. I had to make Cristina believe no one had lived in the house and that it was the ideal place, the house of our dreams. When Cristina saw it, she cried out: "How different it is from the apartments we have seen! Here it smells clean. Nobody will be able to influence our lives or dirty them with thoughts that corrupt the air."

A few days later we got married and moved in there. My in-laws gave us the bedroom set, and my parents the dining-room set. We would furnish the rest of the house little by little. I was afraid Cristina would find out about my lie from the neighbours, but luckily she did her shopping outside the neighbourhood and never talked to them. We were happy, so happy that it sometimes frightened me. It seemed our tranquillity would never be broken in that house of sugar, until a phone call destroyed my illusion. Luckily Cristina did not answer the phone that time, but she might answer it on some similar occasion. The person who called asked for Mrs Violeta: she was no doubt the previous tenant. If Cristina found out that I had deceived her, our happiness would surely come to an end. She wouldn't ever speak to me again, would ask for a divorce, and even in the best possible outcome we would have to leave the house and go live, perhaps, in Villa Urquiza, perhaps in Quilmes, as tenants in one of the houses where they promised to give us some space to build a bedroom and a kitchen. With what? (With junk, for our money was not enough to buy better building material.) At night I was careful to take the phone off the hook, so that no inopportune call would awaken us. I put a mailbox by the gate on the street; I was the only possessor of the key, the distributor of the letters.

Early one morning there was a knock on the door and someone left a package. From my room I heard my wife protesting, then I heard the sound of paper being ripped. I went downstairs and found Cristina with a velvet dress in her arms.

"They just brought me this dress," she said with enthusiasm.

She went running upstairs and put on the dress, which was very tight-fitting.

"When did you order it?"

"Some time ago. Does it fit well? I should wear it when we have to go to the theatre, don't you think?"

"How did you pay for it?"

"Mother gave me a few pesos."

It seemed strange to me, but I didn't say anything, so as not to offend her.

We loved each other madly. But my uneasiness began to bother me, even when I embraced Cristina at night. I noted that her character had changed: her happiness had turned to sadness, her communicativeness to reserve, her calm to nervousness. She lost her appetite. She no longer made those rich, rather heavy desserts out of whipped cream and chocolate that I so enjoyed, nor did she adorn the house from time to time with nylon ruffles, covering the toilet seat or the shelves in the dining room or the chests of drawers or other places in the house, as had been her custom. She would no longer wait for me at tea time with vanilla wafers, or feel like going to the theatre or the movies at night, not even when we were sent free tickets. One afternoon a dog entered the garden and lay down, howling, on the front doorstep. Cristina gave him meat and something to drink; after a bath which changed the colour of his hair, she announced that she would keep him and name him LOVE, because he had come to our house at a moment of real love. The dog had a black mouth, a sign of good pedigree.

Another afternoon I arrived home unexpectedly. I stopped at the gate because I saw a bicycle lying in the yard. I entered without making any noise, then hid behind a door and heard Cristina's voice.

"What do you want?" she repeated twice.

"I've come to get my dog," a girl's voice said. "He passed by this house so many times that he's become fond of it. This house looks as if it's made of sugar. Since they painted it, all of the passersby have noticed it. But I liked it better before, when it was the romantic pink colour of old houses. This house seemed very mysterious to me. I liked everything about it: the bird bath where the little birds came to drink, the vines with flowers like yellow trumpets, the orange tree. Ever since I was eight years old I have wanted to meet you, ever since that day we talked on the phone, do you remember? You promised you would give me a kite."

"Kites are for boys."

"Toys are sexless. I liked kites because they were like huge birds; I imagined flying on their wings. For you it was just a game promising me that kite; I didn't sleep all night. We met in the bakery, but you were facing the other direction and I didn't see your face. Ever since that day I've thought of nothing but you, of what your face looked like, your soul, your lying gestures. You never gave me that kite. The trees told me of your lies. Then we went to live in Moron with my parents. Now I've been back here only a week."

"I've lived in this house for just three months, and before that I never visited this neighbourhood. You must be mistaken."

"I imagined you exactly the way you are. I imagined you so many times! By some strange coincidence, my husband used to be engaged to you."

"I was never engaged to anyone except my husband. What's this dog's name?"

"Bruto."

"Take him away, please, before I get fond of him."

"Violeta, listen. If I take the dog to my house, he'll die. I can't take care of him. We live in a very tiny apartment. My husband and I both work and there isn't anyone to take him out for a walk."

"My name isn't Violeta. How old is he?"

"Bruto? Two years old. Do you want to keep him? I'll visit him from time to time, for I'm very fond of him."

"My husband doesn't like strangers in his house, or for me to accept a dog as a present."

"Don't tell him, then. I'll wait for you every Monday at seven in the evening in Colombia Square. Do you know where it is? In front of Santa Felicitas Church, or if you prefer I can wait for you wherever and whenever you like: for instance, on the bridge by Constitution

Station or in Lezama Park. I'll be happy just to see Bruto's eyes. Will you do me the favour of keeping him?"

"All right. I'll keep him."

"Thank you, Violeta."

"My name isn't Violeta."

"Did you change your name? For us you'll always be Violeta. Always the same mysterious Violeta."

I heard the dull sound of the door and Cristina's steps as she went up the stairs. I waited a little before coming out of my hiding place and pretending I had just come in. Despite the fact that I had witnessed the innocence of the dialogue, I don't know why but a muffled suspicion began gnawing at me. It seemed to me that I had watched a theatrical rehearsal and that the reality of the situation was something else. I did not confess I had witnessed the girl's visit to Cristina. I awaited further developments, always afraid that Cristina would discover my lie and lament that we had moved to this neighbourhood. Every afternoon I passed the square in front of Santa Felicitas Church to see whether Cristina had kept the appointment. Cristina seemed not to notice my uneasiness. Sometimes I even came to believe that I had dreamed it all. Hugging the dog, one day Cristina asked me: "Would you like my name to be Violeta?"

"I don't like flower names."

"But Violeta is pretty. It's a colour."

"I like your name better."

One Saturday, at sunset, I ran into her on the bridge by Constitution Station, leaning over the iron railing. I went up to her and she showed no sign of surprise.

"What are you doing here?"

"Just looking around. I like looking at the tracks from above."

"It's a very gloomy place and I don't like your wandering around alone."

"It doesn't seem so gloomy to me. And why shouldn't I wander around alone?"

"Do you like the black smoke of the locomotives?"

"I like transportation. Dreaming about trips. Leaving without ever leaving. 'Going and staying and by staying leaving.'"

We returned home. Mad with jealousy (jealousy of what? of everything), I barely spoke to her along the way.

"Perhaps we could buy some little house in San Isidro or Olivos; this neighbourhood is so unpleasant," I said, pretending that I had the means to buy a house in one of those places.

"You're mistaken. We have Lezama Park very nearby here."

"It's desolate. The statues are broken, the fountains empty, the trees diseased. Beggars, old men and cripples go there with sacks, to throw out garbage or pick it up."

"I don't notice such things."

"Before, you didn't even like sitting on a bench where someone had eaten tangerines or bread."

"I've changed a lot."

"No matter how much you've changed, you can't like a park like that one. Yes, I know it has a museum with marble lions guarding the entrance and that you played there when you were a girl, but all of that doesn't mean anything."

"I don't understand you," Cristina answered me. And I felt she disliked me, with a dislike that could easily turn to hatred.

For days that seemed like years I watched her, trying to hide my anxiety. Every afternoon I passed the square by the church and on Saturdays went by the horrible black bridge at Constitution Station. One day I ventured to say to Cristina: "If we were to discover that this house was once inhabited by other people, what would you do, Cristina? Would you move away?"

"If other people lived in this house, they must have been like those sugar figurines on desserts or birthday cakes: sweet as sugar. This house makes me feel secure: is it the little garden by the entrance that makes me feel so calm? I don't know! I wouldn't leave here for all the money in the world. Besides, we don't have anywhere to go. You yourself said that some time ago."

I didn't insist, because it was hopeless. To reconcile myself to the idea, I thought about how time would put things back the way they were.

One morning the doorbell rang. I was shaving and could hear Cristina's voice. When I finished shaving, my wife was talking to the intruder. I spied on them through the crack in the door. The stranger had a deep voice and such enormous feet that I burst out laughing.

"If you see Daniel again you'll pay dearly for it, Violeta."

"I don't know who Daniel is and my name isn't Violeta," my wife answered.

"You're lying."

"I don't lie. I don't have anything to do with Daniel."

"I want you to know how things stand."

"I don't want to listen to you."

Cristina covered her ears with her hands. I went into the room and told the intruder to get out. I observed her feet, hands and neck from close up. Then I realized it was a man dressed as a woman. I didn't have time to think what I should do; like a flash of lightning, he disappeared, leaving the door half-open behind him.

Cristina and I never commented on the episode, why I'll never know; it was as if our lips were sealed except for nervous, frustrated kisses or useless words.

It was about that time, such an unhappy time for me, that Cristina suddenly started feeling like singing. Her voice was pleasant, but it exasperated me, because it formed part of that secret world that drew her away from me. Why, if she had never sung before, did she now sing day and night, as she dressed or bathed or cooked or closed the blinds?

One day I heard Cristina say the enigmatic words: "I suspect I am inheriting someone's life, her joys and sorrows, mistakes and successes. I'm bewitched." I pretended not to have heard that tormenting phrase. Nonetheless, I began, God knows why, to learn what I could in the neighbourhood about who Violeta was, where she was, all the details of her life.

Half a block from our house there was a shop where they sold postcards, paper, notebooks, pencils, erasers and toys. For the purpose of my inquiries the clerk at that shop seemed like the best person: she was talkative, curious, and susceptible to flattery. Under the pretext of buying a notebook and some pencils, I went to talk to her one afternoon. I praised her eyes, hands, hair. I did not venture to pronounce the word Violeta. I explained that we were neighbours. I finally asked her who had lived in our house. I shyly said: "Didn't someone named Violeta live there?"

She answered vaguely, which made me even more uneasy. The next day I tried to find out some other details at the grocery store. They told me that Violeta was in a mental hospital and gave me the address.

"I sing with a voice that is not my own," Cristina told me, mysterious once more. "Before, it would have upset me, but now I enjoy it. I'm someone else, perhaps someone happier than I."

Once again I pretended not to have heard her. I was reading the newspaper.

I confess I did not pay much attention to Cristina, since I spent so much time and energy finding out details about Violeta's life.

I went to the mental hospital, which was located in Flores. There I asked after Violeta and they gave me the address of Arsenia Lopez, her voice teacher.

I had to take the train from Retiro Station to Olivos. On the way some dirt got in my eye, so that at the moment I arrived at Arsenia Lopez's house tears were pouring from my eyes as if I were crying. From the front door I could hear women's voices gargling the scales, accompanied by a piano that sounded more like an organ.

Tall, thin, terrifying, Arsenia appeared at the end of a hallway, pencil in hand. I told her timidly that I had come in search of news of Violeta.

"You're the husband?"

"No, a relative," I answered, wiping my tears with a handkerchief.

"You must be one of her countless admirers," she told me, half-closing her eyes and taking my hand. "You must have come to find out what they all want to know: what were Violeta's last days like? Sit down. There's no reason to imagine that a dead person was necessarily pure, faithful, good."

"You want to console me," I told her.

She, pressing my hand with her moist hand, answered: "Yes. I want to console you. Violeta was not only my pupil, she was also my best friend. If she got angry at me, it was perhaps because she had confided in me too much and because she could no longer deceive me. The last days I saw her she complained bitterly about her fate. She died of envy. She constantly repeated: 'Someone has stolen my life from me, but she'll pay for it. I will no longer have my velvet dress; she'll have it. Bruto will be hers; men will no longer disguise themselves as women to enter my house but her house instead; I'll lose my voice, and it will pass to that unworthy throat; Daniel and I will no longer embrace on the bridge by Constitution Station, imagining an impossible love, leaning as we used to over the iron railing, watching the trains go away.'"

Arsenia Lopez looked me in the eye and said: "Don't worry. You'll meet many other women who are more loyal. We both know she was beautiful, but is beauty the only good thing in the world?"

Speechless, horrified, I left that house, without revealing my name to Arsenia Lopez; when she said goodbye, she tried to hug me, to show her sympathy for me.

That day Cristina turned into Violeta, at least for me. I tried following her day and night to find her in the arms of her lovers. I became so estranged from her that I came to view her as a stranger. One winter night she fled. I searched for her until dawn.

I don't know who was the victim of whom, in that house of sugar, which now stands empty.

Visions

Darkness. Non-being. Can anything more perfect exist? Different moments get confused. Sound goes down my throat like a snake. The doctor is at once torturer and jeweller: he bends over me, dazzling me with a flash of intense light. He gives me orders, pierces me, torments me. My body surrenders to him. I am docile. I do not suffer. One has to surrender. I return to the darkness. I return to non-being.

When I am half-awake, the first thing I see is a painting I try to decipher. I think of the very worst English painters, settling on Dante Gabriel Rossetti. This woman, whose hair is lit from behind, is Beata Beatrix. I remember the Latin inscription Rossetti engraved on the frame: QUOMODO SEDET SOLA CIVITAS. Why am I seeing that painting, in light that seems so false? I close my eyes and open them again. It is not a painting. It is a person who is taking care of me, her hair lit up and her face in shadow. The room is dark. When the light is turned on, I look at the room and think it's my own. If I did not leave my house I must be in it, in my room.

The door is on the left; in my room it is on the right. There is a small dark piece of furniture, topped by an oval mirror; in my room there is a large bureau, with a Virgin inside a beacon. The blinds are of wood, and can be raised and lowered with cords; in my room the blinds are of iron and open sideways, in three sections. The electric light in the room is located in a glass square in the centre of the ceiling; in my room there are only two silver standing lamps on the night tables. I am absent-minded. I have lived in this house for so many years without noticing that there are two kinds of blinds in my room: some modern ones that go up and down, made of slats of light wood, and other, old-fashioned ones of heavy iron that open sideways in three sections. I am so absent-minded that I never noticed that there is light not only in the silver standing lamps, but in that square glass lamp on the ceiling, that I never lighted because I never found the switch. Nevertheless I am surprised that I never saw that ground-glass lamp on the ceiling until now; it is very noticeable, now that I am looking at it all the time. Besides, the Virgin beneath the beacon isn't there, or the bureau. The Virgin troubles me. If I were to turn my head back all of a sudden, like an owl, perhaps I would find it. To clean the objects in this room without breaking them, even if they are rarely cleaned (they are always dirty), someone must take them from their usual places and put them somewhere else. The Virgin must be in a corner, under some piece of furniture, or underneath the bedstead. I wonder if a servant cleaned it. But I cannot turn around. Instead of the bureau, which was on a side wall and not across from the bed, I see an amorphous little piece with a small mirror. Am I in Cordoba? Might I be dreaming about Cordoba? There I know of a house with similar furniture. No, I'm not in Cordoba. It must be a present someone gave to me for my birthday, someone who's fond of me but doesn't know what sorts of presents I like. When were those objects brought to my room, and who brought them? They must be very light. Anyone could pick them up and carry them from one place to another. I need not worry. What does it matter who brought them! I could thank any of the people here for this gift I don't like. In case one of them gave it to me, I smile. And that little picture? It's hanging on the wall on the left, above a sort of cot, no doubt a very comfortable one, which I can see from my bed as if I were climbing a mountain. I never saw that cot in my room, nor in any other room in my house. Furniture has its own life; it's not strange that the pieces go in and out, change places, are replaced by others whenever they feel like it. Isn't it better that way? What's wrong with this room? Is it worth saying something about it to someone? Perhaps I should speak to the first person who approaches:

the nurse. Her apron crackles: it's very starched, so starched that it looks as if it were made of plaster, if plaster could gleam. This woman enjoys being a nurse. What a shame that the others don't enjoy their work as much as she does. She's happy. Sometimes a quick little dog follows her around, but I can't see it very well.

But before I can question her, the nurse answers me with a question: "Don't you know where you are, dear?"

"No."

"In the hospital, dear."

"Oh, that's why."

"What?"

"Why I didn't recognize my room."

"Don't be frightened."

How short life would be if some unpleasant moments didn't make it interminable! In a room that's not my own, for hours and hours I have believed that it is mine and tried to figure out where I am—and I don't die!

Like the architect who finds the lost plans of a house, or the navigator or explorer who guides himself by a compass that seems broken, or better still like an animal that's settling into a new lair and trying to remember the one before, I calm down and, to calm myself more completely, investigate where the hospital is, whether the window of my room faces the river, how long I've been here.

Noises fill my surroundings with their perverse stories. What's that saw that starts screeching early in the morning? Does it chop up human beings? Does it grind their bones until it turns them to sand? Do they use that material to build houses? And that noise like boiling water coming up from the basement and ground floor? Is it the sound of lips praying, or the boilers of hell where boiling liquids are prepared for sinners? In a hospital? The voices were like the buzzing of flies. Are they the same ones? And a roaring like that of wild animals from the people in the hallways: what will it turn into? Into monsters in distress, or a procession of men with costumes improvised from torn sheets or wet towels, traveling toward the desert, carrying inedible, stinking provisions. There are so many days of carnival when it is not carnival!

These faces appear etched against the darkness. All of a sudden I see them. They can be distinguished from the furniture but seem to be of the same material. They are the faces of the doctors. They have hands but no bodies or souls. Crowding together they come toward me. It is they who suffer. They are the next victims. Those who suffer, suffer less than those who watch their suffering.

They suddenly turn on a light, as if they wanted to surprise me in the middle of some unspeakable sin. One of them, a cross between a god and a locomotive, has a light on his specialist forehead.

They sit me down, hit me, uncover me, shout at me, poke me, stick a thermometer in me, push their fingers into my abdomen until I cry out, tickle me with a blood-pressure gauge on my arm.

"Breathe," they tell me. "Don't breathe," they say, until I turn purple.

How many patients must have died in the hospital because of the examinations! I don't want to think about it. Such violent treatment could kill even healthy people, but perhaps it would save them because it would keep them from falling asleep. After all, sleep foreshadows death.

Because of the many interruptions, time stretches out. The clock looks at me, its face round and ashen. It is eternal like the sun: its hours do not shoot out like bolts of lightning.

Eight visits a day by the doctors turn a day into a year. Should we be grateful that something so unpleasant allows us to measure time?

The serum falls drop by drop. An hourglass egg timer, a water-clock in a lost garden in Italy, are less obsessive. There is something feverish about the falling sand, the falling water. The needle stuck in our vein turns into our vein. I don't look at it.

I don't like the grey steel veins of the machines. I am like a machine, but human veins are a different colour. Blue, blue. Ink, blood. Blue ink and red blood look alike.

There are floods in Buenos Aires. I know it because I can feel it. I know it from the newspapers (without reading them): I can hear them crackling in the next room.

It's the birthday of some sort of queen. It is nighttime. I can hear the drums celebrating the event. People gather in a square with impro-vised altars and play the famous symphony on wind instruments. How odd that I never heard it before! The music of a band comes from the river and ever more excitedly intones a sublime melody. I would prefer not to use the word "sublime" for any piece of music. But what other word could be used to designate that one? On the highest note, that enters all ears as if it were a long needle, people are so disturbed that the tremulous sound vibrates, endlessly prolonged . . . How could I have never heard such a well-known melody before? There must be many recordings of it conducted by different symphony conductors, modified with different rhythms.

The deaf children in the square, as if they recognize the melody, swing back and forth frantically. They do not kneel before the improvised altars, for they are much too nervous. The children are the lucky ones. That music lasts the whole night. It's like a curse. How dramatic it is, how long, how endless! At dawn, solitary men on the pink terraced roofs whistle it, confused by the intonation, since they don't know it well. I don't know at what solemn, diaphanous moment the last vibration of that music disappears: music in whose dawn the day never arrives, as ejaculation is endlessly postponed in yogis' pleasure. A few hours later, colours, then astonishing visions, burst on my dazzled eyes. Suddenly a yellow hue fills my sight, one never seen before. Like a neon sign it traces its figure on light purple water (the purple seeming to indicate water). Inside the yellow zone (representing the earth), groups of motionless, grey, fearful people are clearly etched, as if carved in stone, beneath countless parasols, like the Buddha's parasols, saving themselves from something. From what? It occurs to me that this is a map of the world, filled up with monuments.

In the next room someone is reading the news of the floods in the papers. I once knew a dog that slept on newspaper. The crackling of the paper, when it moved around or breathed hard, made me think it was reading the news.

A spot of dampness appears on the wall where the head of my bed rests. I look for it without luck in the mirror that faces me. It disturbs me. I know that it is green, purple, blue, like a bruise, and that it's getting larger. Could it be a symbol of my sickness? That spot of dampness hurts me as if it were inside my body. They call a man to look at it. I wonder if he is a plumber. He carries a little brown bag. The man pokes, bangs on the wall, pays no attention to me. He sighs.

I am thinking of Blake's illustrations to the *Book of Job* and the *Gates of Paradise*.

"There's nothing that can be done," he exclaims, and leaves the room together with his smell of putty. "Every year it's the same. It comes from the house next door," he adds, coming back into the room.

The nurse gives me something to drink. The water doesn't taste like water.

"Enjoy your meal," the plumber says to me.

They call a sister of charity. The sister of charity comes: she slides along in her dark skirt and her happy, doll-like face as if rolling on little wheels. She is of the opinion that pipes are mysterious. The house will have to be torn down to find out where the dampness comes from. She leaves the room with her keys and rosaries.

They used to take presents to the dead. I wonder if I am dead. They bring me a fragrant bouquet of passion flowers, two green nightgowns, candy that is much too sweet, hearts made of chocolate, a bouquet of roses that makes me sick, a pot of cyclamen that I give to the Virgin, a box of cookies, soup that nauseates me.

There are cars in the street, a phone in the room. What time of year is it? Nowadays everything is taken away from dead people: the rings and teeth, because they are gold; the eyes, because the cornea is used in other eyes; the skin or hair, because they're used for grafts and wigs. They haven't taken anything from me: I am not dead.

What's going on outside? I have to find out. Trees keep on growing, getting ready for new seasons. The awful monument with a pink marble pedestal and bronze women I can glimpse through the window here will no doubt always have those yellow stripes belonging not to the marble but to the piss of passing dogs or nocturnal men with diuretic loves.

"Do you want me to adjust your pillow?"

When I entered this mansion, the winter fortunately had already pulled the leaves from the trees and autumn, my favourite season because of its golden fruit, had fled.

"Do you want a glass of water?" they ask me.

The smooth, glossy, soft rottenness of the public parks, where men go for fresh air or to masturbate, is nearby. When they open the window that dirty wind comes in, giving the illusion of cleanliness because it's cold now in wintertime. There are people who sit down, who are sitting, on the benches: women who knit while looking at their own children or at other people's; beggar women with bundles of clothing or containers of old bread smelling like oranges; men who press against human beings or plants alike with the same passion to tell secrets; well-cared-for or lost dogs; hysterical cats that copulate, filling the night with electric cries.

"Some fruit juice?" a sugary voice asks.

"How did I get here?" I ask.

"In an ambulance," they tell me.

"And how did they bring me?"

"In the stretcher, up the elevator."

I arrived in the darkness, like a mouse in a basement, without dreaming, stiff, without any sensation, still. When I was a girl I played statues, always with the fear of turning into a statue; I played in a dark room (an aphrodisiacal game), afraid of disappearing. You had to close your eyes.

"This time," I am thinking, "I played statues in the dark in all seriousness."

The araucaria, sooty and huge, and the unreal rubber tree are nourished on excrement, semen, and glass. Nobody waters them, except God when it rains. All things, even trees, have a will to live, above all and in spite of everything. But if the form of one individual passes on to another, if nothing is lost, why struggle so hard to preserve a given form that, in the final account, might be the most inferior or the least interesting!

"What's your name?" I ask the nurse.

"Linda Fontenla."

Linda Fontenla likes to talk; she also likes the seriousness of the sick. What is a healthy person? A boring good-for-nothing. For Linda Fontenla life is an endless series of enemas, thermometers, transfusions, and poultices skillfully distributed and applied. If she gets married, she'll marry a sick man, for such a person would be attractive to her, a bundle of hemorrhoids, an enlarged liver, a perforated intestine, an infected bladder, or a heart full of extrasystoles.

"Believe it or not, an old man I was taking care of wanted to go to bed with me. Some people have no shame. He offered me everything, even marriage. I told him to go peddle his wares somewhere else. That's why I don't like taking care of men. They're all the same. You can't even apply talcum powder to them; you can take my word for it. They want to enjoy themselves, that's all they want."

"Am I dying, Linda?"

"Dear, what nonsense you talk. Do you want me to bring you the little hand mirror so you can see how well you look? Here you are. Look at yourself. Yesterday you were in bad shape. I was very much afraid."

"But yesterday you told me that I was very well."

"You have to be told that so you'll perk up a little."

I look at myself in the hand mirror, but at the same time look at the nurse's hand. Nurses have so many painted nails, many more than other people.

"I have a sheep face," I hear my voice saying, as if it were someone else's.

"Like a sheep? Your face looks like a sheep face to you? How funny you are!"

"That sheep face sick people have."

"It's the first time I've ever heard that."

"You must know it, though."

"Don't talk so much. It's bad for your heart."

I look at the palm of my hand.

"They told me you can read palms," Linda continues. "Would you read mine someday?"

"If I don't die."

"Always the same thing! Always death. You should think about happy things. Do you want me to tell you a story? When I arrived this morning, a group of women was crying and praying in the entrance hall. I thought to myself: *Rats, my patient died.* It was the man next door, you see? Who would have guessed? Their faces were three yards long from crying. They would scare anyone."

"But couldn't they have been crying for me?"

"There wasn't anybody from your family, or any of your friends. Calm down. Are you going to be suspicious now?"

"I don't care in the slightest."

"I know. It was just a joke."

"Turn off the light."

I'm absorbed in my visions. Once again I look at the shadows of the room interwoven with brilliant colours. At first it's a paradise for my eyes. I venture forward with fear, as happens when one is in love. May nobody speak to me or interrupt me. I am present at the most important moment of my life. On the white wall of the room the history of the world unrolls. I have to decipher the signs, at times very complicated ones. The planisphere has begun, with yellow earth, purple water, and groups of people with profiles like bison, sheltered beneath countless parasols. What images await me now? They change as if by magic. I see a head gazing out of a window. The window is composed of four large stones. The head is beautiful, almost angelic one might say, until the stones at the top and the bottom begin to close. The mouth laughs, showing its teeth, like the masks in Greek tragedy. The colours fade. An expression of pain appears on the face: the stones are grinding the frightened, frightening face. I wish to see some other vision. I bring them about. How? I have a supernatural power, but a limited one. I do not always succeed in seeing beautiful or reassuring things. Don't I like seeing Blake's drawings? These visions seem to come from the *Book of Los* or the *Gates of Paradise*. An endless series of black horses with gleaming harnesses covers the wall. I don't know what carriages these horses are hitched to, nor to what distant century they correspond. They dazzle me so much that I cannot focus on what surrounds them. Muffled bells accompany their slow march. An indescribable joy comes with them. How sad it would be if these horses never return! Now they vanish like clouds in the western sky. They were so precise, so clear! To where did they flee? These visions must be like certain skies that are never repeated. Now, walking along at the same pace as the horses, as if their limbs were moving in water, four harlequins are going around in circles. There are many other harlequins; the room is full of harlequins, but these four catch my attention. I wish they'd never go away! Horses sometimes make me afraid; they are black; at times they are gloomy, funereal. These figures, on the other hand, could never be anything but harlequins, light, happy, immaterial. Looking at them is like making love endlessly, like discovering perfection, like being in heaven. But as I look at them I foresee that they will disappear, and that nothing will be able to replace them.

The inside of a room appears, filled with happy characters who form part of some unknown world; then, outside now, an enormously tall staircase made of climbing legs appears against the blue sky. And when I'm convinced they will not return, the harlequins appear, moving their bodies as slowly as is possible only in water. An irrepressible joy seizes me. They come back because I desire so strongly that they do so. Has my supernatural power been perfected? But now they vanish and mystical figures replace them: first the Apostles and then Jesus Christ. Jesus, with a crown of thorns on Saint Veronica's veil, but then the beautiful face of Jesus turns into the face of a monkey and I look aside, to the right. I see a chest of drawers right before my eyes: a shiny mahogany chest I'll never open. The chest changes when I stop looking at it. Now it's an ordinary varnished cedar chest with white spots on it. I don't want to look to my left. Before me I now see a garden covered with huge vines growing up to the sky, and among these vines there are marble statues, also growing skyward. Later I see a mountain of stone gleaming, but notice the stones are people who are being crushed together, who are killing each other, people of stone who kill one another with stones. The mountain grows as the dead accumulate; the stone men reproduce.

A white lion shines, filling the whole wall.

When someone comes into the room and turns on the light, the visions disappear, but the ceiling is covered with the most beautiful roses or with stripes of all the colours of the rainbow.

A long-legged dancer is carrying the square glass of the lamp (like a shield) in his hands; he takes it away from the centre of the ceiling, but then returns and puts it back in the middle again. I stop looking at the ceiling to admire the roses, prominent against the endless foliage. I never saw roses stand out against the sky with such intensity. I see them come closer as if viewed through several magnifying lenses. Then they get smaller, becoming almost imperceptible once again, and more beautiful. The light in the next room goes out. The angel appears. A Chinese garden gradually appears, as slowly as if by a transfer process. I look at this image from every possible angle, as if collecting postcards for an album. I am afraid it will disappear. If I could write a date, a name, underneath it I would do so. It disappears. Nothing will console me now that it has disappeared. It was a fathomless garden guarding a pagoda. Bamboo was waving back and forth, no doubt in the wind, and there was shade and lakes and rivers with motionless canoes. Everything perfectly still!

I see a golden ship with a million heads looking over the gunwale; it's not moving forward, or if it moves it moves with me on a blue sea. It's a Greek ship. Carrying men's heads as if they were fruit, fruit without bodies, fruit with faces, all the same size, all of them bald.

Now the people have suddenly grown old, the joy has turned to pain, the goodness to cruelty, the beauty to ugliness. Why? Nothing lasts. Why? Am I suffering? Is each face a symbol of what I am feeling without knowing it?

There is an angel I am waiting for. He is not here; he was not present in my visions. I hear his step, I feel his hand; he gives me something to drink, something to eat. I'm saving images for him, little figures like those which children glue in their notebooks. I hope he likes them! A painting, a book, would not please me nearly as much!

Beauty has no end or edges. I wait for it. But where is my bed, where I can wait in comfort? I'm not lying down; I am unable to do so. A bed is not always a bed. There is the birthing bed, the bed of love, the deathbed, the riverbed. But this one is not a real bed...

The Wedding

That a young woman of Roberta's age should pay attention to me, go out for walks with me, confide in me, was a source of joy that none of my friends could share. She had control of me, and I loved her, not because she gave me candy or marbles or coloured pencils, but because she sometimes spoke to me as if I were big and sometimes as if both of us were six years old.

The control Roberta exerted over me was mysterious: she said I guessed her very thoughts and desires. She was thirsty: I would bring her a glass of water she had not asked me for. She was hot: I fanned her or brought her a handkerchief moistened in cologne. She had a headache: I offered her an aspirin or a cup of coffee. She wanted a flower: I gave it to her. If she had given me an order—"Gabriela, jump out of the window" or "put your hand in the coals" or "run on the railroad tracks so the train will hit you" —I would have obeyed instantly.

We all lived on the outskirts of the city of Cordoba. Arminda Lopez was my next-door neighbour and Roberta Carma lived across the street. Arminda Lopez and Roberta Carma loved each other like cousins, which is what they were, but at times addressed one another rather harshly: that happened especially when they were talking about clothes or underwear or hairdos or boyfriends. They never thought about their jobs. Half a block from our houses was the LOVELY WAVES beauty salon. Roberta took me there once a month. While they bleached her hair with peroxide and ammonia, I played with the stylist's gloves, with the spray, combs, hairpins, with a hair dryer that looked like a warrior's helmet, and with an old wig the hairdresser very kindly let me use. That wig pleased me more than anything in the world, more than the walks to Ongamira or the Sugarloaf, more than fruit pastries or the bluish horse that crossed the vacant lot when it was wandering around the block, without reins or saddle, distracting me from my studies.

Arminda Lopez's engagement distracted me more than the beauty parlour or the strolls. I got bad grades, the worst in my whole life, during those days.

Roberta took me by streetcar to the Oriental coffee shop. There we had hot chocolate with vanilla wafers and a young man came up to talk to her. On the way back in the tram Roberta told me that Arminda was luckier than she was because at twenty, women had to fall in love or throw themselves in the river.

"Which river?" I asked, disturbed by these confidences.

"You don't understand. How could you? You're still very young."

"When I marry, I'm going to have a beautiful chignon," Arminda said. "My hairdo will catch every eye."

Roberta laughed and protested: "How old-fashioned. Nobody wears chignons anymore."

"You're wrong. They're in fashion again," Arminda answered. "You'll see, everybody will look at me."

The preparations for the wedding were long and painstaking. The gown was sumptuous. A piece of fine lace from her maternal grandmother adorned the dress, while a piece of lace from the paternal grandmother (so that she would not be jealous) adorned the veil. The dressmaker had Arminda try on the dress five times. Kneeling, her mouth full of pins, the dressmaker adjusted the hem or added pleats to the top of the dress. Holding her father's arm, Arminda crossed the patio of her house five times, entering her bedroom and stopping in front of a mirror to see what effect the pleated dress made as she moved. The hairdo was perhaps what most worried Arminda. She had dreamed about it all her life. She had an enormous chignon made with a lock of hair she had had cut off when she was fifteen. A delicate golden net with little pearls held the chignon together; the hairdresser showed it off in his shop. According to her father, her chignon looked like a wig.

On the wedding morning, the second of January, the thermometer stood at 105 degrees. It was so hot that we didn't have to moisten our hair before combing it or rinse our faces with water to take off the dirt. Exhausted, Roberta and I were on the patio. It was getting dark. The sky, of a leaden grey, scared us. The storm turned out to be only a lot of lightning and millions of bugs. A huge spider was sitting in the vine in the patio: it seemed to me it was looking at us. I took a broomstick to kill it, but something stopped me. Roberta cried out: "It represents hope. A French lady once told me that 'a spider in the evening means hope.' "

"Then, if it means hope, let's keep it in a little box," I said.

Moving like a sleepwalker because she was tired (because she is good), Roberta went to her room to look for a box.

"Be careful. They're poisonous," she said.

"And if it bites me?"

"Spiders are like people: they bite to defend themselves. If you don't do anything to them, they won't do anything to you."

I opened a little box in front of the spider, and in a single hop it jumped inside. Afterwards I closed the top, making air holes in it with a pin.

"What are you going to do with it?" Roberta asked.

"Keep it."

"Don't lose it," Roberta answered.

From then on, I walked around with the box in my pocket. The next morning we went to the beauty salon. It was Sunday. They were selling blankets and flowers in the street. Those joyful colours seemed to celebrate the nearness of the wedding. We had to wait for the hairdresser, who had gone to Mass, while Roberta sat under the dryer.

"You look like a warrior," I shouted.

She didn't hear me and kept on reading her missal. Then I felt like playing with Arminda's chignon, which lay beside me. I took off the hairpins which held the locks together under the beautiful hair net. It seemed to me that Roberta was looking at me, but she was so absent-minded that she just stared into space, as if staring fixedly at someone.

"Shall I put the spider inside?" I asked, showing her the chignon.

No doubt the noise of the hair dryer prevented her from hearing my voice. She did not answer me, but nodded her head as if in agreement. I opened the box, turned it upside down in the chignon, and the spider fell inside. Then I quickly rearranged the hair, putting back the fine netting and the pins so they would not catch me by surprise. Doubtless I did it skillfully, because the hairdresser didn't notice anything unusual in his work of art, as he himself termed the bride's chignon.

"All of this will be a secret between us," Roberta said, as we left the beauty shop, twisting my arm until I cried out. I couldn't recall what secrets she had told me that day and I answered the way I'd heard adults talk.

"I'll be silent as the grave."

Roberta put on a fringed yellow dress, and I wore a white starched dress with plumes and a lace insert. In the church I didn't look at the bride because Roberta told me you didn't have to look at her. The bride was very pretty with a white veil full of orange blossoms. She was so pale she looked like an angel. Then she fell down, senseless. From afar she looked like a curtain that had been released. Many people went up to help her, fanning her, going to the chancel for water, patting her face. For a time they thought she had died; for another while they thought she was alive. They carried her to her house, cold as marble. They didn't want to undress her or take off her chignon before putting her in the coffin. Shyly, awkwardly, ashamed of myself, I accused myself, during the two days of the wake, of having been the cause of her death.

"How did you kill her, you lousy kid?" asked a distant relative of Arminda, who drank coffee incessantly.

"With a spider," I answered.

My parents held counsel to decide whether they needed to call a doctor. Nobody ever believed me. Roberta took a dislike to me; I think she felt repelled by me and never went out with me again.

Voice on the Telephone

No, don't invite me to your nephews' house. Children's parties depress me. That probably seems silly to you. Yesterday you got angry because I didn't want to light your cigarette. Everything is connected. So I'm crazy? Maybe. Since I can never see you, I'm going to end up explaining things on the phone. What things? The story of the matches. I hate the phone. Yes. I know you love it, but I would have preferred to tell you all that in the car, or on the way out of the movie theatre, or in a coffee shop. I have to return to the time of my childhood.

"Fernando, if you play with matches, you'll burn the house down," my mother would tell me, or perhaps: "The whole house is going to be reduced to a little pile of ashes," or maybe: "We will all fly away like fireworks."

Does that seem normal to you? That's what I think too, but all that made me want to touch matches all the more, to caress them, to try to light them, to live for them. The same thing happened with you and erasers? But they didn't forbid you to touch them. Erasers don't burn. You ate them? That's different. The memories of when I was four years old tremble as if illuminated by fire. The house where I spent my childhood, as I told you already, was huge: it had five bedrooms, two entrance halls, two living rooms with ceilings painted with clouds and

95

little angels. You think I lived like a king? No, you're wrong. There were always fights between the servants. They were divided into two groups: the supporters of my mother and the followers of Nicolas Simonetti. Who was he? Nicolas Simonetti was the cook: I was crazy about him. He threatened me, in jest, with a huge shiny knife, gave me little slices of meat and lettuce leaves to play with, gave me caramel I spilled on the marble floor. He contributed as much as my mother did to awakening my passion for matches, lighting them so I could blow them out. Because of the supporters of my mother, who were tireless, the food was never ready, or tasty, or done properly. There was always a hand that intercepted the plates and let them cool, that added talcum powder to the noodles, that dusted the eggs with ashes. All of this culminated with the appearance of a tremendously long hair in the rice pudding.

"That hair is Juanita's," my father said.

"No," said my aunt, "I don't want to 'get in her hair,' to my taste it's Luisa's."

My mother, who had a great deal of pride, got up from the table in the middle of the meal and, grasping the hair between her fingertips, carried it to the kitchen. My mother was annoyed by the face of the cook, entranced, who saw it not as a hair but as a strand of black thread. I don't know what sarcastic or wounding phrase made Nicolas Simonetti take off his apron, wrap it up in the shape of a ball as if to throw it, and announce that he was leaving the household. I followed him to the bathroom where he got dressed and undressed each day. That time, he who was so attentive to me dressed without looking at me. He combed his hair with a bit of grease he had left on his hands. I never saw hands that so resembled combs. Then, with dignity, he gathered up the moulds, enormous knives, and spatulas in the kitchen, put them in the briefcase he always carried, and went toward the door with his hat on. To make him look at me I gave him a kick in the shins; he put his hand, which smelled of lard, on my head, saying: "Goodbye, kid. Now, many people will be able to appreciate Nicolas's food. They'll lick their lips."

You think that's funny? I'll keep on with my list: there were two studies. Why so many? I ask myself the same thing; nobody wrote. Eight hallways, three bathrooms (one with two sinks). Why two? Perhaps they washed with four hands. Two stoves (one inexpensive, the other electric), two rooms for washing and ironing (my father said one was so the clothes could get wrinkled), a pantry, a vestibule by the dining room, five servants' rooms, a room for the trunks. Did we travel so much? No. Those trunks were used for many different things. Another room was for chests of drawers; another, for odds and ends, was where the dog slept and where my hobbyhorse sat on a tricycle. Does that house still exist? It exists in my memory. The objects are like milestones showing you how far you've gone: the house had so many of them that my memory is full of numbers. I could say what year I ate my first apple or bit the dog's ear, or when I pissed in the candy dish. You think I'm a pig! I preferred the rugs, chandeliers, and glass cabinets in that house to my toys. For my birthday my mother organized a party. She invited twenty boys and twenty girls so they would bring me presents. My mother had foresight. You're right, she was a sweetheart! For the party, the servants took out the rugs, and my mother replaced the objects in the glass cabinets with little cardboard horses filled with surprises and little plastic cars, rattles, cornets and piccolos for the boys, and bracelets, rings, change purses and little hearts for the girls. In the middle of the dining table they put a cake with four candles, sandwiches and chocolate milk. Some children arrived (not all of them with presents) with their nursemaids, others with their mothers, others with an aunt or a grandmother. The mothers, aunts or grandmothers sat down to chat. Standing in the corner, blowing on a cornet that made no sound, I listened to them.

"How pretty you are today, Boquita," my mother said to the mother of one of my girlfriends. "Did you come from the country?"

"It's the season of the year when you want to get a little burned and you end up looking like a monster," Boquita answered.

I thought she was referring to fire rather than to the sun. Did I like her? Who? Boquita? No. She was horrible, with a tiny mouth, no lips, but my mother said that you should never compliment the pretty ones for their beauty, but instead the ugly ones because that was good manners; she said beauty was of the soul and not of the face; that Boquita was a fright, but "had something." Besides, my mother didn't lie: she always managed to utter the words in an equivocal way, as if her tongue got stuck, and that's how she said "how petty you are, Boquita," which could also be taken as a compliment due to her friend's strong personality. They spoke of politics, of hats and clothes, of economic

problems, of people who had not come to the party: I assure you that
I'm repeating the exact words I heard them say. After the balloons
were passed out, after the puppet show (in which Little Red Riding
Hood terrified me as much as the wolf did the grandmother, in which
the Beauty seemed as horrible as the Beast to me), after blowing out
the candles on my birthday cake, I followed my mother into the most
private room in the house, where she shut herself in with her friends,
surrounded by embroidered pillows. I managed to hide behind an
armchair and trample on a lady's hat, squatting down, leaning against
a wall so as not to lose balance. You know I'm no fool. The ladies were
laughing so much I could hardly understand what they were saying.
They spoke of bodices, and one of them unbuttoned her blouse to her
waist to show the one she had on. It was as transparent as a Christmas
stocking; I thought it must have some toy inside it and yearned to stick
my hand in. They spoke of sizes: it turned out to be a game. They took
turns standing up. Elvira, who looked like a huge baby, mysteriously
took a tape measure out of her pocketbook.

"I always carry a nail file and a tape measure in my pocketbook, just
in case," she said.

"What a madwoman," Boquita shouted boisterously; "you look like
a dressmaker."

They measured their waists, busts and hips.

"I bet you my waist is a twenty-two."

"I bet you mine is less."

Their voices echoed as in a theatre.

"I would like to win with my hips," one said.

"I would be happy winning with my bust," another one said. "Men
are more interested in breasts, haven't you seen them staring?"

"If they don't look me in the eye I don't feel anything," said another
one, who had a sumptuous pearl necklace.

"It's not a matter of what you feel, it's what they feel," said the ag-
gressive voice of one woman who wasn't anyone's mother.

"I couldn't care less," the other answered, shrugging her shoulders.

"Not me," said Rosca Perez, who was beautiful, when it was her turn
to be measured; she bumped against the armchair where I was hiding.

"I won," said Chinche, who was as pointed as a small-headed pin,
shaking the nine silver bangles she wore on one arm.

"Twenty," Elvira exclaimed, examining the tape measure that was wrapped around Chinche's tiny waist.

Who would have a twenty-inch waist, except maybe a wasp? So she must have been a wasp. Could she make her stomach go down like a yogi? She was no yogi, but she was a snake charmer. She fascinated women who were perverted. Not my mother. My mother was a saint. She felt sorry for her. When people gossiped about Chinche she would comment: "A crock of nonsense."

One day. I had never heard her call a scoundrel "a crock of nonsense." It must have been something personal. That was very typical of her. I'll go on with my story. At that moment the phone rang by one of the armchairs. Chinche and Elvira answered it together. Then, covering the receiver with a pillow, they told my mother: "It's for you, dear."

The others jostled one another, and Rosca took the phone to hear the voice.

"I bet it's the one with the beard," one of the ladies said.

"I bet it's the elf," said another, chewing on her necklace.

Then a phone conversation began in which all of them took part, passing the phone along from one to the next. I forgot I was supposed to be hiding and stood up to watch the ladies' enthusiasm, marked by the ringing sounds of bracelets and necklaces. When my mother saw me, her voice and expression changed. As if she were in front of the mirror she smoothed her hair and pulled up her stockings; she then carefully put out her cigarette in the ashtray, twisting it two or three times. She took me by the hand and I, taking advantage of her confusion, stole the fancy long matches that were on the table next to the whisky glasses. We left the room.

"You have to attend to your guests," my mother said severely. "I'll attend to mine."

She left me in the dismantled living room, without a carpet, without the usual objects in the glass cabinet, without the most valuable furniture, and filled instead with hollow horses made of cardboard, with cornets and piccolos on the floor, with little cars with owners who seemed like impostors to me. Each of the children was hugging and pulling at a balloon in an alarming way. On top of the piano, which was covered with cloth, someone had put all of the presents my friends had brought me. Poor piano? Why don't you instead say poor Fernando! I noticed that some presents were missing, for I had carefully counted and examined them as soon as I received them. I thought they must be somewhere else in the house and so began wandering through the hallway that led to the garbage can, where I dug out some cardboard boxes and pieces of newspaper. These I triumphantly took back to the dismantled living room. I discovered that some of the children had taken advantage of my absence to take possession once more of the presents they had brought me. Smart? Shameless. After much hesitation and many difficulties in dealing with the children, we sat down on the floor to play with some matches. A nursemaid came by and told her companion: "There are very fine decorations in this house: there are flower vases that would squash your foot if they fell on it." Looking at us as if she were speaking of the same vases, she added: "Each one alone is a devil, but together they're like the baby Jesus."

We made buildings, plans, houses, bridges out of matches; for a long while we twisted their heads. It was not until later, when Cacho arrived with his glasses on and a wallet in his pocket, that we tried lighting the matches. First we tried to light them on the soles of our shoes, then later on the stones of the chimney. The first spark burnt our fingers. Cacho was very wise and told us that he knew not only how to prepare, but how to light, a bonfire. He had the idea of enclosing the vestibule next to the dining room, where his nursemaid was, with fire. I protested. We should not waste matches on nursemaids. Those fancy matches were destined for the private room where I had found them. They were the matches belonging to our mothers. On tiptoe we approached the door to the room where we could hear voices and laughter. I was the one who locked the door with the key; I was the one who took the key out and put it in my pocket. We piled up the paper in which the presents had been wrapped, and the cardboard boxes full of straw; also some newspaper that had been left on a table, the bits of trash I had collected, and some pieces of firewood from the chimney, where we sat for a moment to watch the future bonfire. We heard Margarita's voice, saying: "They have locked us in." I have not forgotten her laughter.

One of them answered: "That's better, that way they'll leave us alone."

At first the fire hardly threw off any sparks, then it exploded, growing like a giant, with a giant's tongue. It licked the most expensive piece of furniture in the house, a Chinese chest with lots of little drawers, decorated with millions of figures who were crossing bridges, looking out of doorways, walking along the banks of a river. Millions and millions of pesos had been offered to my mother for that piece, and she had never wanted to sell it at any price. You think that's a shame? It would have been better to sell it. We moved back to the front door where the nursemaids had gathered. The voices calling for help echoed down the long service staircase. The doorman, who was chatting at the streetcorner, did not arrive in time to operate the fire extinguisher. They made us go down to the courtyard. Bunched together under a tree, we saw the house in flames, and the useless arrival of the firemen. Now do you understand why I refused to light your cigarette? Why matches make such an impression on me? Didn't you know I was sensitive? Naturally, the ladies gathered by the window, but we were so interested in the fire that we barely noticed them. The last vision I have of my mother is of her face pointed downward, leaning against the balcony railing. And the Chinese chest of drawers? The Chinese chest was saved from the fire, luckily. Some little figures were ruined: one was of a lady who was carrying a child in her arms, who slightly resembled my mother and me.

Icera

When Icera saw the set of doll furniture in the window of that enormous toy store at the Colon Bazaar, she coveted it. She didn't want it for her dolls (she didn't have any) but for herself, because she wanted to sleep in that tiny wooden bed, whose frame was decorated with garlands and baskets of flowers, and to look at herself in the mirror of the wardrobe, which had tiny drawers and a door that locked. She wanted to sit in the little chair with a cane seat and a turned back, in front of the dressing table, with an extra bar of soap, and a comb to tame her rebellious hair.

The head of the doll department, Dario Cuerda, took a liking to the girl.

"She's so ugly," he would say, by way of excusing his attentions to her to the other employees.

Icera considered the dolls as rivals; she didn't accept them even as presents: she wanted only to occupy the place they occupied. Because she was stubborn, she stuck firmly to her ideas. This peculiarity of character, more than her height (she was much shorter than is normal), called attention to her. The girl always went with her mother to look at toys, but not to buy them, since they were very poor. The head of the doll department, Dario Cuerda, let Icera lie down in the little bed, look at herself in the little mirror of the wardrobe, and sit in the chair, in front of the dressing table, to comb her hair, just the way the lady across the street from her house did.

Nobody gave Icera any toys, but for Christmas Dario Cuerda gave her a dress, a little hat, gloves, and doll shoes, all of which had been damaged and so could be sold only at a discount. Icera, mad with joy, went out wearing her new clothes. She still has them.

The little girl caused Cuerda some difficulties with her visits, because if allowed to choose a present she always chose the most expensive one.

"Mr Cuerda is always so generous," the other employees at the store would say to the regular customers.

His reputation for generosity cost him a fair amount of money. The girl liked practical toys: sewing and washing machines, a grand piano, a sewing kit with all the tools, and a trunk with trousseau, all of which cost a fortune. Dario Cuerda gave her a guitar and a rake; then, since there were not many inexpensive toys, he chose to give her soaps, hangers, and little combs, things that made the girl happy because they were of some use.

"Children grow up," Icera's mother would say, sincere and unhappy. "What mother isn't secretly sorry to see her daughter grow, even though she'd like her to grow taller and stronger than the other girls!" Icera's mother was like all mothers, only perhaps a little poorer and a little more devoted. "Some day, this little dress will no longer fit you," she would continue, showing her the little doll dress. "What a shame! I once was little too, and look at me now."

Icera would look at her mother, who was inconsolably tall. Children grew up, it was true. Few things in the world were so true. Ferdinando wore long pants, Prospera could not find shoes her size, Marina didn't climb trees because, given her height (she resembled a giraffe), they were too short for her. A tiny distress gnawed for several days at Icera's heart, but she decided that if she repeated the words, "I won't grow up, I won't grow up" ceaselessly to herself, she would halt her deceptive growth. Besides, if she wore the doll dress, gloves and hat every day, she would necessarily continue to be the same size. Her faith worked a miracle. Icera did not grow.

Then she fell ill, and for four weeks was unable to get dressed. When she got up she had grown four inches. She felt a great loss, as if that increase had diminished her. And in fact it had. She was no longer allowed to stand on the table; she no longer had her baths in the washtub; wine was no longer given to her in her mother's thimble; the grapes she was given and the *macachines* she gathered in the countryside no longer took up as much space in the palm of her hand. The dress, gloves and shoes no longer fit her. The hat perched on top of her head. Anyone would find it easy to imagine the girl's displeasure: just remember how annoyed you feel when you get fat, when your feet or face swell, when the fingers of your gloves get wrinkled like raw sausages. But by looking hard enough she found solutions for these problems: the dress became a blouse; the gloves could be made into mittens; by cutting off the heels the shoes could be used as slippers.

Icera lived happily once again, until an ill-intentioned person reminded her of her misfortune.

"How you've grown!" said a wretched neighbour.

To show that it was not true, Icera tried hiding under the ferns in the yard, but three other neighbours discovered her right away, and kept on talking about her abnormal height.

Icera ran to the toy store, her place of refuge. Her heart filled with bitterness, she stopped in the doorway. That day only dolls were exhibited in the shop window. The odious dolls, with their stiff smell of hair and new clothes, gleamed behind the glass, among the reflections of admiring passers-by who streamed along Florida Street. Some dolls were dressed for first Communion, some as skiers, others as Little Red Riding Hood, others as schoolgirls; only one was dressed as a bride. The bride-doll was a little different from the one dressed for first Communion: she carried a little bouquet of orange blossoms in her hand and was enclosed in a light-blue cardboard box, like a candy box. Icera, forgetting her normal shyness, went into the toy store looking for Dario Cuerda. She asked the other employees where he was, since she couldn't find him in his usual place.

"Mr Dario Cuerda?" (Icera, usually so silent, was forgetting her shyness.) "Would you please call him?" she said to one of the employees whom she most feared.

"Here he is," the cashier said, pointing to an old man who looked like Dario Cuerda disguised as an old man.

Dario Cuerda was so covered with wrinkles that Icera did not recognize him. On the other hand he, with his blurry memory, remembered her because of her height.

"Your mother used to come and look at the toys. How she liked the bedroom sets and the little sewing machines!" Dario Cuerda said politely, moving forward with a maternal tenderness. He noticed that the little girl had whiskers and false teeth. "These modern young people," he exclaimed; "the dentists treat them like adults."

How wrinkled we all are! thought Dario Cuerda. Later on he imagined that it was all a dream, a product of his fatigue. *So many old faces, so many new faces, so many chosen toys, so many sales receipts with carbon copies to write while the customer gets impatient. So many children growing old and old people turning into children!*

"I have to tell you a secret," said Icera.

For Icera's mouth to reach Dario Cuerda's extremely long ear, the little girl had to climb up on the counter.

"I am Icera," Icera whispered.

"Your name is Icera too? That's normal. Children are named after their parents," said the head of the doll department, thinking to himself: *Old age obsesses me: even children look old to me.* (In his mind he amused himself mispronouncing the words.)

"Mr Cuerda, I would like you to give me the box for the bride-doll," Icera whispered, tickling him unbearably on the ear.

Icera had never spoken such a long or well-pronounced sentence. In her view, that box would assure her future happiness. Getting it was a matter of life or death.

"Everything is passed on," Cuerda exclaimed, "especially predilections. There is practically no difference between this girl and her mother. This girl speaks better but looks like an old woman," he added, addressing someone he thought was Icera's grandmother, who looked like a ghost.

Icera thought that when she got into that box she would stop growing. But she also thought that she would have a sort of revenge against all the dolls in the world by taking away this box, lined with blue lacy paper, from the most important of them all. Dario Cuerda, straining against his fatigue, since it was no small job to take something from the display window, untied all the ribbons that held the doll in the box, and gave the box to Icera.

Just at that moment an unexpected photographer walked by, carrying the tools of his trade. When he saw a crowd of people gathered in the Colon Bazaar, he discovered that Icera, for whom he had been searching for some time, was in the toy store. The photographer asked permission to take a picture, while Icera got comfortable inside the box and Cuerda tied the ribbons over her. He knelt down on one knee, brandished his camera, moved farther away, and moved closer again as if he were himself a doll. Perhaps that picture would be good publicity for the shop, Cuerda thought proudly. As he smiled, he forgot his wrinkles and those of the little girl, blinded by the flash that illuminated them.

The photographer, who worked for a newspaper, began taking notes, consulting the old woman who accompanied Icera. This was just a formality, as he already knew the name, address and age of the girl, her life and its miracles.

"When did your daughter turn forty?" he asked.

"Last month," Icera's mother responded.

Then Dario Cuerda realized that what was happening was not the result of his fatigue. Thirty-five years had passed since Icera's last visit to the Colon Bazaar. He thought, confusedly perhaps (because he was in fact extremely tired), that Icera had not grown more than four inches in all that time because she was destined to sleep future nights in that box, which would prevent her growing in the past.

The Autobiography of Irene

I never felt so passionately eager to see Buenos Aires lit up on Independence Day, for sales at department stores festooned with green streamers, or for my birthday, as I was to arrive at this moment of supernatural joy.

Ever since I was a girl I've always been as pale as I am now, "perhaps a little anemic," the doctor would say, "but healthy, like the whole Andrade family." On several occasions I imagined my death, while sitting before mirrors and holding a paper rose. Now I have that rose in my hand (it was in a vase by my bed). A rose, a vain ornament smelling like a rag, with a name written on one of its petals. I don't need to smell it, to look at it: I know it's the very same one. Today I am dying, and my face is the very one I saw in the mirrors of my childhood. (I have hardly changed. Accumulated weariness, crying and laughter have made my face more mature, forming and deforming it.) Every dwelling place will seem old and familiar to me.

The unlikely reader of these pages will ask for whom I am telling this story. Perhaps the fear of not dying forces me to do so. Perhaps I write for myself: to read it over, if by some curse I should keep on living. I need evidence. I am distressed only by the fear of not dying. In truth I think that the only sad part about death, about the idea of death, is knowing that it cannot be remembered by the person who has died, but solely, and sadly, by those who watched that person die.

My name is Irene Andrade. I was born twenty-five years ago in this yellow house, with balconies of black wrought iron and bronze plates bright as gold, six blocks from the church and square of Las Flores. I am the oldest of four rambunctious children in whose childhood games I took a passionate part. My maternal grandfather was French; he died in a shipwreck that rendered the eyes of his portrait, venerated by guests in the shadows of the living room, misty and mysterious. My maternal grandmother was born in this town, a few hours after the first church burned down. Her mother, my great-grandmother, told her all the details of the fire that had hastened her birth. She passed those stories on to us. No one was better acquainted with that fire, with her own birth, with the main square sowed in alfalfa, with the death of Serapio Rosas, with the execution of two prisoners in 1860 near the atrium of the old church. I know my paternal grandparents only through two yellowing photographs, obscured by a kind of respectful haze. They look more like brother and sister than husband and wife; more like twins than mere siblings. They had the same thin lips, the same curly hair, the same detached hands resting idly on their laps, the same fond docility. My father, who revered the education he had received from them, raised plants: he was as gentle with them as he was with his children, giving them medicines and water, covering them with canvas on cold nights, giving them the names of angels, and finally, "when they had grown," selling them with utmost regret. He would caress the leaves as if they were the hair of a child; I think that in his later years he talked to them, or at least that was the impression I had. All of this secretly annoyed my mother. She never told me as much, but in the tone of her voice, when she told her friends—"Leonardo is in there with his plants! He loves them more than his children!"—I guessed a perpetual mute impatience, the impatience of a jealous woman. My father was a man of average height, with beautiful, regular features, dark complexion and chestnut hair, and an almost blond beard. No doubt it is from him that I have inherited my seriousness, the admirable suppleness of my hair, the natural goodness of my heart, and my patience, a patience that might almost seem a fault, a sort of deafness, a bad habit. My mother, when she was younger, embroidered for a living: that sedentary life had filled her as if with still water, somewhat cloudy yet at the same time tranquil. No one rocked so elegantly in the rocker, no one handled fabric so eagerly. Now, she has that perfect kind of affectation that old age provides. In her I see only maternal whiteness, the severity of her gestures and voice: there are voices that you can see, that keep on revealing the expression of a face even after its beauty is gone. Thanks to that voice I can still discover whether her eyes are blue or her forehead high. From her I must have inherited the whiteness of my skin, my fondness for reading or needlework, and a certain proud, disdainful shyness toward those who, even when they are shy, might be or at least seem to be modest.

Without bragging I can say that until I was fifteen, at the very least, I was the favourite at home because I was older and was a girl: circumstances most parents, who prefer boys and the younger children, would not have found appealing.

Among the most vivid memories of my childhood I shall mention: a shaggy white dog named Jasmine; a Virgin four inches tall; the oil painting of my maternal grandfather which I have already mentioned; and a vine with trumpet-shaped orange flowers, called bignonia or War Trumpet.

I saw the white dog in a kind of dream and later, more insistently, in my waking hours. I would tie him to the chairs with a rope, would give him food and water, would pet and punish him, would make him bark and bite. My loyalty to an imaginary dog, at the very time I scorned other more modest but more real toys, made my parents happy. I remember they would point at me proudly, telling the guests: "Look how she can entertain herself with nothing." They would frequently ask me about the dog, asking me to bring him into the living room or, at meal times, into the dining room; I obeyed enthusiastically. They pretended to see a dog that only I could see; they praised or teased him, to please or distress me.

The day my parents received a shaggy white dog from my uncle in Neuquen, nobody doubted that the dog's name was Jasmine or that my uncle had been a partner in my games. However, my uncle had been away for more than five years. I did not write to him (I barely knew how to write). "Your uncle is a seer," I remember my parents saying at the moment they showed me the dog: "Here is Jasmine!"

Jasmine recognized me without surprise; I kissed him.

Like a sky-blue triangle, with golden borders, the Virgin began taking shape, acquiring density in the remoteness of a June sky. It was cold that year and the windows were dirty. I wiped them with my handkerchief, opening up little rectangles on the window panes. In one of those rectangles the sun lit up a cloak and a formless, tiny, round, red face that seemed sacrilegious to me at first. Beauty and saintliness were for me two inseparable virtues. I lamented the fact that her face was not beautiful. I cried for many nights, trying to alter it. I remember that this apparition impressed me more than that of the dog, because at that time I had a tendency toward mysticism. Churches and saints exerted a fascination on my spirit. I prayed secretly to the Virgin, offering her flowers, gleaming candies in little liqueur glasses, tiny mirrors, perfumes. I found a cardboard box about her size; with ribbons and curtains I turned it into an altar. At first, when she watched me pray, my mother smiled with satisfaction; later, she was disturbed by the intensity of my fervour. I heard her tell my father, one night by my bed, when they thought I was asleep: "Let's hope she doesn't turn into a saint! Poor thing, she doesn't bother anyone! She's so good!" She was also disturbed to see the empty box in front of a pile of wild flowers and votive candles, thinking that my fervour was leading to some sacrilege. She tried to give me a St Anthony and a St Rose of Lima, relics that had belonged to her mother. I did not accept them; I told her that my Virgin was dressed in blue and gold. I showed her the size of the Virgin with my hands, explaining timidly that her face was small and red, sunburned, without any sweetness of expression, like the face of a doll, but shining like that of an angel.

That same summer, at the market where my mother did her shopping, the Virgin appeared in a shop window: it was the Virgin of Lujan. I did not doubt that my mother had ordered it for me, nor was I surprised that she had exactly guessed the shape and colour of the Virgin, the form of the mouth. I remember she complained of the price, because it was damaged. She brought it home wrapped in newspaper.

My grandfather's painting, that majestic ornament of the living room, caught my attention when I was nine years old. Behind a red curtain, which made the image stand out all the more, I discovered a frightening, dark world. Children sometimes find pleasure in such worlds. Deep, dark, vast expanses like green marble were trembling there, broken, icy, furious, tall, with forms like mountains here and there. Next to that painting I felt cold, tasted tears on my lips. Along wooden hallways, women with long hair and men in distress were fleeing, standing motionless. There were a woman covered with an enormous cape and a man whose face I never saw who walked, holding hands with a child carrying a hobbyhorse. It was raining somewhere; a tall flag was waving in the wind. That treeless landscape, so similar to the one I could see at dusk from the streets at the edge of town—so similar and at the same time so different—disturbed me. One summer day, sitting in an armchair, alone, in front of the painting, I fainted. My mother said that when she woke me up I asked for water with my eyes closed. Thanks to the water she gave me, with which she cooled my brow, I was saved from an unexpectedly premature death.

One day at the end of spring, in the courtyard of our house, I saw the vine with orange flowers for the first time. When my mother sat knitting or embroidering, I would push off the boughs (which only I could see) so that they would not get in her way. I loved the orange colour of the petals, the warlike name (which was confused with the history lessons I was studying at that time), and the light scent, like rain, given off by the leaves. One day, my brothers heard me utter its name and began speaking of San Martin and his grenadiers. In the endless afternoons, the gestures I made to pull the boughs from my mother's face, so they would not bother her, seemed intended to scare off the flies that sit aggressively still in certain points in space. Nobody foresaw the future vine. An inexplicable apprehensiveness prevented me from speaking of it before it arrived.

My father planted the vine in the very spot in the courtyard where I had anticipated its opulent form and colour. It was in the very place where my mother would sit. (For some reason, perhaps because of the sun, my mother could not sit in any other corner of the courtyard; for some reason, perhaps for the very same reason, the vine could not be planted anywhere else.)

I was judicious and reserved. I'm not praising myself: these secondary virtues sometimes give rise to grave faults. Because of vanity or lack of physical strength, I was more studious than my brothers. No lesson seemed new to me. I enjoyed the quiet that books afford. I enjoyed, above all else, the astonishment caused by my extraordinary facility for all kinds of study. Not all of my girlfriends liked me, and my favourite companion was solitude, which smiled on me during recess. I read at night, by candlelight. (My mother had forbidden me to read because it was bad, not only for the eyes but also for the brain.) For a time I studied the piano. The teacher called me "Irene the euphonious," and this nickname, which I did not understand and which my classmates repeated with sarcasm, offended me. I thought that my stillness, my apparent melancholy, and my pale face had inspired the cruel nickname: "the cadaverous." To make jokes about death seemed to me to be in poor taste for a teacher; and one day, crying, because I already knew how mistaken and how unfair I could be, I made up a slander against that young lady, who had only wanted to praise me. Nobody believed me, but she, one afternoon when we were alone in the living room, took me by the hand and said: "How can you repeat such intimate, such unfortunate things!" It was not a reproach: it was the beginning of a friendship.

I may have been happy; I was until I was fifteen. The sudden death of my father brought about a change in my life. My childhood was ending. I tried to use lipstick and high heels. Men looked at me at the train station, and I had a boyfriend who waited for me on Sundays at the door of the church. I was happy, if happiness exists. I enjoyed being an adult, being beautiful, with a beauty criticized by some of my relatives.

I was happy, but the sudden death of my father, as I said before, brought about a change in my life. Three months before he died, I had already prepared my mourning and the black crepe; I had already cried for him, leaning majestically on the balcony railing. I had already written the date of his death on a print; I had already visited the cemetery. All of that was made worse by the indifference I showed after the funeral. To tell the truth, after his death I never remembered him at all. My mother, good as she was, could never forgive me for that. Even now she looks at me with that same expression of rancour that for the first time awoke in me the desire to die. Even now, after so many years, she cannot forget the mourning worn in advance, the date and name written on a print, the unexpected visit to the cemetery, my indifference to this death at the very core of a large family in distress. Some people looked at me with suspicion. I could not hold back my tears when I heard certain bitter, ironic phrases, usually accompanied by a wink. (Only then did oblivion seem like bliss to me.) They said I was possessed by the devil; that I had wished for my father's death so that I could wear mourning and a clasp of jet; that I had poisoned him so as to be able to spend my time at dances and at the train station without worrying about his proscriptions. I felt guilty for having unleashed such hatred around me. I spent long sleepless nights. I managed to get sick but was unable to die, as I had desired.

It had not occurred to me that I might have a supernatural gift, but when beings stopped being miraculous for me, I felt miraculous toward them. Neither Jasmine nor the Virgin (now broken and forgotten) existed. An austere future awaited me; my childhood grew more distant.

I felt guilty for the death of my father. I had killed him when I imagined him dead. Other people did not have this power.

Guilty and unlucky, I felt capable of infinite future joys, which only I could invent. I had projects for my happiness: my visions should be pleasant, I should be careful with my thoughts and try to avoid sad ideas, try to invent a happy world. I was responsible for everything that happened. I tried to avoid images of drought, floods, poverty, illnesses of people at home or of my acquaintance.

For a time that method seemed effective. But very soon I understood that my intentions were as vain as they were childish. At the entrance to a store I was forced to watch two men fight. I refused to see the secret knife, I refused to see the blood. The struggle looked like a desperate embrace. It occurred to me that the death agony of one of them and the gasping terror of the other were a final reconciliation. Without being able to erase the horrible image even for a moment, I was forced to witness the death in all its sharpness, the blood mixed with the dirt of the street, a few days later.

I tried to analyze the process, the form in which my thoughts developed. My visions were involuntary. It was not hard to recognize them; they always appeared in the company of certain unmistakable signs, always the same ones: a slight breeze, a curtain of mist, a tune I cannot sing, a door of carved wood, a clammy feeling in my palms, a little bronze statue in a distant garden. It was useless to try to avoid these images: in the icy regions of the future, reality rules.

I then understood that to lose the ability to remember is one of the greatest of misfortunes, since events, though infinite in the memory of normal beings, are extremely brief, indeed almost nonexistent, for one who foresees them and then merely lives them. Those who do not know their destinies invent and enrich their lives with hopes of a future that will never turn out that way. That imagined destiny, prior to the real one, exists in a sense, and is as necessary as the other. The lies my girlfriends spoke sometimes seemed truer than the truth. I have seen expressions of bliss on the faces of people who live on hopes that are always frustrated. I think that the essential lack of memories, in my case, did not proceed from a lack of memory: I think that my thought, so busy with seeing the future, so full of images, did not have time to dwell on the past.

Leaning out on the balcony, I would see the children on their way to school going by with the faces of grownups. That made me shy of children. I could see the future afternoons full of conversations, rosy or lilac clouds, births, terrible suffering, ambition, unavoidable cruelty against human beings and animals.

Now I understand to what an extent I viewed events as final memories. They replace memories so inadequately. For instance: if I were not about to die, then this rose, at this moment in my hand, would not live in my memory; I would lose it forever in a tumult of visions of a future destiny.

Hidden in the shadow of courtyards, of hallways, in the icy atrium of the church, I meditated constantly. I tried to take charge of my memories of my girlfriends, of my brothers, of my mother (because they were the most substantial ones). It was then that the touching vision of a forehead, of some eyes, of a face, began to haunt and pursue me, forming my desires. That face lingered for many days and many nights before taking shape. The truth is: I had the burning desire to be a saint. I vehemently wished for that face to be that of God or of the infant Jesus. In church, in prints, in books, and in medallions I searched for that adorable face: I didn't want to find it anywhere else, didn't want it to be human, or contemporary, or true.

I think nobody has ever had so much trouble recognizing the danger signs of love. How I gave in to my adolescent tears! Only now can I remember the light, yet penetrating, aroma of the roses Gabriel gave me, while gazing into my eyes, as we left school. That prescience would have lasted a whole lifetime. In vain I tried to delay meeting Gabriel. I could foresee separation, absence, oblivion. In vain I tried to avoid the hours, paths, and places that were propitious for that meeting. That prescience should have lasted a whole lifetime. But destiny put the roses in my hands and put the real Gabriel before me without surprise. My tears were useless. Uselessly I copied the roses on paper, writing names and dates on the petals: a rose can be invisible forever in a rose garden, before our window, or in the lover's hand that offers it to us; only memory will preserve it intact, with its perfume, its colour and the devotion of the hands that offer it.

Gabriel was playing with my brothers, but when I would appear with a book or with my sewing basket and sit down on a chair in the courtyard, he would leave his games to offer me the homage of his silence. Few children were as astute. He made little airplanes of flower petals, of leaves. He hunted fireflies and bats, and tamed them. From watching the movements of my hands so much, he learned to embroider. He embroidered without blushing: architects made house plans; he, when he embroidered, made plans of gardens. He loved me: at night, in the dark courtyard of my house, I could feel his involuntary love growing with all the naturalness of a plant.

Without knowing it, how I hoped to penetrate the chaste memory of those moments! Without knowing it, how I yearned for death, the only keeper of my memories! A hypnotic fragrance, the rustling of eternal leaves on the trees, comes to guide me along the paths, now so long forgotten, of that love. Sometimes an event that seemed labyrinthine to me, slow to develop, almost infinite, can be expressed in two words. My name, written in green ink or with a pin, on his arm, on him who filled six months of my life, now fills only a single sentence. What is it to be in love? For years I asked the piano teacher and my girlfriends. What is it to be in love? To remember a word, a look within the density of other spaces; to multiply and divide and transform them (as if they were displeasing to us), to compare them, unceasingly. What is a beloved face? A face that is never the same, a face that is transformed without end, a face that disappoints us . . .

A silence of cloisters and roses was in our hearts. No one could guess the mystery that joined us. Not even those coloured pencils or the jujube candies or the flowers he bestowed on me gave us away. He would write my name on the trunks of trees with his penknife, and when he was being punished he would write it with chalk on the wall.

"When I die I will give you candies every day and will write your name on all the tree trunks in heaven," he once told me.

"How do you know we'll go to heaven?" I answered. "How do you know there are trees and penknives in heaven? Are you sure that God will allow you to remember me? Are you sure that in heaven your name will be Gabriel and mine Irene? Will we have the same faces, and recognize each other?"

"We'll have the same faces. And even if we didn't, we would recognize each other. That day of Carnival, when you dressed up as a star and spoke with an icy voice, I recognized you. With my eyes closed, I've seen you many times since then."

"You've seen me when I wasn't there. You've seen me in your imagination."

"I saw you when we were playing nurse and patient. When I was the one who was wounded and they were blindfolding my eyes, I guessed when you were coming."

"Because I was the nurse, and I had to come. You could see me under the blindfold: you were cheating. You always cheated."

"In heaven I'll recognize you without cheating. I'd recognize you even in disguise, I'd see you coming with my eyes blindfolded."

"Then you believe there'll be no difference between this world and heaven?"

"Only what bothers us will be missing: part of the family, bedtime hours, some penance, and the moments when I don't see you."

"Perhaps it's better in hell than in heaven," he said to me another day, "because hell is more dangerous and I like suffering for you. To live amid flames, because of your fault, to save you continually from the demons and fire, would be a source of joy for me."

"But do you want to die in mortal sin?"

"Why mortal and not immortal? Nobody forgets my uncle: he committed a mortal sin and they didn't give him the last rites. My mother told me, 'He is a hero; don't listen to what people say.'"

"Why do you think about death? Usually young people avoid such sad, harmful topics of conversation," I protested one day. "Right now you look like an old man. Look at yourself in a mirror."

There was no mirror nearby. He looked at himself in my eyes.

"I don't look like an old man. Old men comb their hair in a different way. But I'm already grown up, and acquainted with death," he answered. "Death is like absence. Last month, when my mother took me to Azul for two weeks, my heart stopped, and in my veins, sadly, I felt coursing, not blood, but cold water. Soon I will have to go farther away for an indefinite time. I console myself imagining something simpler: death or war."

Sometimes he lied to move me to pity: "I'm sick. Last night I fainted in the street."

If I criticized him for lying, he'd answer: "One only lies to people one loves: truth leads to so many mistakes."

"I'll never forget you, Gabriel": the day I told him that I had already forgotten him.

Without distress, without weeping, already accustomed to his absence, I withdrew from him before he went away. A train pulled him from my side. Other visions already separated me from his face, other loves, less touching farewells. I last saw his face through the pane of the train window, sad and in love, erased by the superimposed images of my future life.

It was not for lack of amusements that my life turned sad. Once I confused my own destiny with that of a character in a novel. I should confess: I confused the face of an illustration I foresaw with a real face. I waited for some dialogues that I later read in a book, in an unknown city in 1890. The antiquated clothing of the characters did not surprise me. "How fashions are going to change," I thought with indifference. The figure of a king, who didn't look like a king because he showed only his face in the plate of a history book, devoted his fond glances to me in the autumn twilight. Before, the texts and characters of books had not appeared to me as future realities; it's true that up until then I'd not had the chance to see many books. The books belonging to one of my grandfathers were stored in a room at the back of the house; bound with twine, wrapped in spider webs, I saw them when my mother decided to sell them. For several days we inspected them, dusting them with rags and feather dusters, gluing in the loose pages. I read in the moments I was alone.

Far from Gabriel, I understood by a miracle that only death would let me recover his memory. The afternoon when no other visions, no other images, no other future disturbed me would be the afternoon of my death, and I knew I would wait for it with this flower in my hand. I knew that the tablecloth I would embroider for months on end, with yellow daisies and pink forget-me-nots, with garlands of yellow wisteria and a gazebo surrounded by palm trees, would be used for the first time the night of my wake. I knew that this tablecloth would be praised by the guests who had made me weep ten years before. I heard the voices, a chorus of female voices, repeating my name, disfiguring it with sad adjectives: "Poor Irene," "unfortunate Irene!" Then I heard other names, not people's names but those of little cakes and plants, uttered with pained admiration: "What delightful palm trees," "what madeleines!" But then with the same sadness, and with the insistence of a psalm, the chorus repeated: "Poor Irene!"

The false splendour of death! The sun lights up the same world. Nothing has changed when everything has changed for only one being. Moses foresaw his own death. Who was Moses? I thought that no one had ever foreseen his own death. I thought that Irene Andrade, this modest Argentine woman, had been the only one in the world capable of describing her death before she died.

I lived waiting for the limit of life that would draw me closer to memory. I had to put up with infinite moments. I had to love the mornings as if they were definitive; I had to love certain shadows in the main square, Armindo's eyes; I had to get sick from typhus fever and cut my hair. I met Teresa, Benigno; I came to know the Fountain of Love and the Sentinel in Tandil. In Monte, in the railroad station, I drank tea with milk, with my mother, after visiting a lady who taught needlework and knitting. In front of the Garden Hotel I saw the death agony of a horse that looked as if he were made of clay. (He was abused by flies and a man with a whip.) I never went to Buenos Aires: some calamity always prevented the trip I had planned. I never saw the dark outline of the train in Constitution Station. Now I never will. I will have to die without seeing Palermo Park, the Plaza de Mayo all lit up and the Colon Theatre with its boxes and its desperate artists singing with their hands on their breasts.

I agreed to being photographed against a sad backdrop of trees with a beautiful tall hairdo, wearing gloves and a straw hat decorated with red cherries, so battered they looked real.

I slowly carried out the last episodes of my destiny. I will confess that I was oddly mistaken when I foresaw the photograph of myself: although I found it similar, I didn't recognize my own image. I felt indignant with that woman who, without neglecting my imperfections, had usurped my eyes, the position of my hands and the careful oval of my face.

For those who remember, time is not too long. For those who wait it is inexorable.

"In a small town everything is quickly over. There won't be any new houses or new people to meet," I thought, trying to console myself. "Here death arrives more quickly. If I had been born in Buenos Aires, my life would have been interminable, my sorrows would never end."

I remember the solitude of the afternoons when I sat in the square. Would the light hurt my eyes so I would weep for something besides sorrow? "She's thirty years old and has still not married," some glances told me. "What is she waiting for," others said, "sitting here in the square? Why doesn't she bring her sewing? Nobody loves her, not even her brothers. When she was fifteen she killed her father. The devil possessed her, God knows in what form."

These dreary, monotonous visions of the future depressed me, but I knew that in the rarefied space of my life, where there was no love, no faces, no new objects, where nothing happened any more, my torment was coming to its end and my happiness was beginning. Trembling, I was coming closer to the past.

The cold of a statue took possession of my hands. A veil separated me from the houses, drew me away from the plants and people: nonetheless I saw them clearly outlined for the first time, minutely present in their every detail.

One January afternoon, I was sitting on a bench by the fountain in the square. I remember the stifling heat of the day and the unusual coolness brought on by the sunset. Somewhere, surely, it had rained. I had my head resting on my hand; in my hand was a handkerchief: a sad posture, sometimes inspired by heat, and at that moment inspired by sorrow. Someone sat down next to me. She spoke to me with a woman's soft voice. This was our dialogue:

"Excuse my impertinence. There isn't time for formal introductions. I don't live in this town; chance brings me here from time to time. Even if I sit down sometime in this square again, it's unlikely that our conversation will be repeated. Perhaps I'll never see you again, not even in a store, or on a railway platform, or in the street."

"My name is Irene," I replied. "Irene Andrade."

"Were you born here?"

"Yes, I was born and will die in this town."

"I never thought of dying in a particular place, no matter how sad or enchanting it might be. I never thought of my death as a possibility."

"I didn't choose this town to die in. Destiny assigns places and dates without consulting us."

"Destiny decides things but doesn't take part in them. How do you know you'll die in this town? You're young and you don't look sick. One thinks of death when one is sad. Why are you sad?"

"I'm not sad. I've no fear of dying and destiny has never disappointed me. These are my final afternoons. These pink clouds will be the last ones, with their shapes like saints, like houses, like lions. Your face will be the last new face; your voice will be the last one I hear."

"What has happened to you?"

"Nothing has happened to me and, happily enough, few things have still to happen to me. I have no curiosity. I don't want to know your name, I don't want to look at you: new things disturb me, delay my death."

"Haven't you ever been happy? Aren't certain memories full of hope for you?"

"I have no memories. The angels will bring me all my memories the day of my death. The cherubim will bring me the forms of all the faces. They will bring me all the hairdos and ribbons, all the positions of arms, the forms of hands in the past. The seraphim will bring me the taste, the sound and the fragrance, the flowers I received as presents, the landscapes. The archangels will bring me the dialogues and farewells, light, the silence of reconciliation."

"Irene, it seems to me that I've known you for a long time! I've seen your face somewhere, perhaps in a photograph, with a tall hairdo, ribbons of velvet, and a hat decorated with cherries. Isn't there a picture of you like that, with a sad backdrop of trees? Didn't your father sell plants a long time ago? Why do you want to die? Don't lower your eyes. Don't you admit the world is beautiful? You want to die because everything becomes more definitive and more beautiful at times of parting."

"For me death will be a time of arrival, not of parting."

"Arriving is never pleasant. There are people who could not arrive even in heaven feeling happy. One must get used to faces, to the places one has most loved. One must get used to voices, to dreams, to the sweetness of the country."

"I'll never arrive anywhere for the first time. I recognize everything. Even heaven sometimes scares me. The fear of its images, the fear of recognizing it all!"

"Irene Andrade, I'd like to write your biography."

"Ah! If you could help me cheat my destiny by not writing my biography, what a favour you would do me. But you will write it. I can already see the pages, the clear handwriting, and my sad destiny. It will begin like this:

I never felt so passionately eager to see Buenos Aires lit up on Independence Day, for sales at department stores festooned with green streamers, or for my birthday, as I was to arrive at this moment of supernatural joy.

Ever since I was a girl I've always been as pale as I am now...

The Sibyl

The tools of my trade are in the police station: gold wristwatch, gloves, piece of wire, wooden box with lock and key, flashlight, pliers, screwdriver and briefcase (to look more serious I always carry a brief-case). Weapons? I never wanted them. What are my hands for? I say. They are iron claws; if they don't strangle, they punch as God wills them to.

Lately I've felt discouraged. There's so much competition and poverty. Everyone knows that! The life of a butcher is less toilsome than ours. At night, I felt no desire to go walking around blocks to get acquainted with some particular neighbourhood of Buenos Aires or a certain house; I felt utterly bored. In the northern part of the city, I liked Palermo because of its fountains and lakes, places where one can drink and wash the nails of several fingers; in the southern part of the city, I liked Constitution, no doubt because there I met my com-rades on the escalator while going up and down, down and up, devoted to our profession. I sat in the squares, eating oranges or bread, or, when I was lucky, salami or cream cheese. Sometimes the passers-by looked at me as if they noticed something strange about me. I don't wear a beard to my navel, or go around with my toenails showing, or have enormous birthmarks between my eyebrows, or gold teeth. The other day I asked one of them, "Do I have two noses?" forgetting my responsibility, my age, my situation. Perhaps my blue flannel pants are loud because they have a zipper instead of buttons in the crotch. Everything you do to avoid calling attention to yourself ends up calling attention. What can you do? If I slide along like a worm, everybody notices how I walk. If I dress like a pig, the colour of trees or walls or dirt, everyone looks at my clothing. If I try not to raise my voice, God help me, everybody strains to hear me. Eating ice cream is impossible for me. The girls watch me and nudge one another with their elbows. Sometimes it's not pleasant to be nice to women; I have to hear idiotic remarks all day long. Luckily I can no longer hear out of one ear. I turned deaf at sixteen. They punctured my eardrum with a splinter. We lived with my parents in Punta Chica, in a house built on pilings. One night, when I had put catfish in their beds as a joke, my father, who is always in a foul mood, and my brothers, who are grouches, plucked up courage and held me down on the floor. While the others held me, one of them stuck the splinter into my ear. Afterwards, naturally, so that I wouldn't talk, they put me in a sack and threw me in the river. The neighbours saved me. It seemed strange to me. Later I found out that they did it to make me talk. People are so curious! Everybody hates me, except for women; nevertheless, Miss Romula, who lives in the store, summoned me one day because I had killed a cat with a kick on the head near the door of her room. "You boor," she said, "can't you do such things somewhere else?"

How could a few drops of blood on the floor bother her? They can be wiped up in a couple of seconds. She never forgave me. She's lazy, that's what she is. When they hired me at the Firpo Drugstore, people started staring at me as if I was a guy who attracts attention. "Slug-gard," they called me when I ran, "Express Train" when I walked slow-ly, "Pigpen" when I had bathed, "Palmolive" when I hadn't. But what most infuriated me was when they called me "Pizza," unfairly, because they saw me one day, while I was making deliveries on my bicycle, eating a piece of Paschal cake that Susana Plombis had given me to carry in my pocket in case I felt hungry.

It was then that I got to know the interiors of many houses. None of them made such an impression on me as that of Anibal Celino; it must be because I came in through the front door. In the other houses I had to enter through the kitchen. I still have some spoons, some silver salt shakers, that I took from the drawers while the servants were looking for money to pay the bill, things that were of no use to me. Anibal Celino's house was a palace, nothing less. The first time they sent me there was with a package from the Firpo Drugstore; the service door looked like the front door and I went looking for the other one, thinking that it was the service door, because it was dirty. I'm well acquainted with the houses of today. A very luxurious house is a dirty house. The door was closed but it opened when I pushed the door knocker, a bronze lion biting on a ring, also of bronze. I went into the house and couldn't see anyone. I went out again and there in the garden I saw the unkempt wigs of the palm trees. What trees! Not even a dog could like them. I went back in: there was nobody there. The door opened by itself. I bumped right into a marble staircase with a balustrade as shiny as the lion on the door knocker. I walked a few steps and entered an enormous room full of glass cabinets; it looked like a store or a church. All around I saw statues, candy dishes, miniatures, necklaces, fans, reliquaries, dolls. Already, in my hand, because I am very absent-minded, I saw a candy dish of gold with turquoise inlay; I put it in my pocket. Later I put a little figurine that was glittering on a table in my other pocket. (My pockets have double bottoms, in case of need. Rosaura Pansi is in charge of lining them. I give her lots of presents and the poor thing is so grateful it's embarrassing.) When I left the living room I heard a little noise on the staircase, maybe a mouse. My heart stopped, for I saw a very young girl, sitting on the top stair, watching me with a mischievous expression. She made me laugh.

"I have a package from the Firpo Drugstore," I told her.

"What a shame!" she answered. "Then you are not the Lord."

"So I'm not a gentleman? What am I, then? I've brought a bottle of rubbing alcohol, milk of magnesia and rice powder," I said, reading the bill.

"This isn't the service entrance. Go out," she said, taking the bill from me and looking at it. "Go to the corner. There they will assist you."

I would have liked to strangle that girl; she was as white and smooth as the porcelain angel I once saw in the showcase of a religious articles store.

"Aren't all the doors the same?"

"All of them," she replied, "except the door to heaven."

"So why don't you accept the package and pay for it?"

"Because I don't have money to pay bills. I have money to give away or to lose."

"To give to whom?"

"To give to anybody who's not a member of my family or one of my friends."

"And how do you lose it?"

"Lose it? In a thousand different ways."

She took a change purse full of silver coins from the pocket of her smock and lined the coins up in a row along the step.

"Coins are lost when you play with them to read a fortune," she said, "in fountains or wherever; what matters is that they disappear. What good are they?"

She seemed a little less repulsive to me and I said to her: "Goodbye, Kitty."

"My name is Aurora," she answered with an authoritarian tone.

"Is it my fault that you have the eyes of a cat? Are you angry?"

She did not answer me and ran skipping up the staircase.

For a long time I did not see Aurora again, no matter how often I went to the house to make deliveries.

When they fired me at the Firpo Drugstore, I met Penknife and Lathe. We understood one another, I can't say as if we were brothers, considering the row I had with my own brothers; we understood one another as if we were inseparable friends. That is to say, many times we couldn't look one another in the eye without bursting out laughing, even when we were surrounded by people. The truth is that everything was a game. I soon told them about Anibal Celino's house and about Aurora, one day when we were walking down Canning Street. I listed the objects I had seen there. It was a real inventory! None of the valuable things in that palace had escaped my notice. Penknife looked at me, discouraged: "What a lot of junk! What good is it to us?" he said.

But Lathe's eyes lit up. Sharper than Penknife, he whispered, with that voice of his that sounded like a whistle in the dark: "We'll go in there some time this week."

We each had eight ice-cream cones and then went to the zoo to look at the monkeys. The sun was burning hot. We stopped to listen to the music of a merry-go-round, because Lathe likes all kinds of music. That's not surprising: his father played the concertina. As if his mind were on something else, he was planning the break-in.

For several days, as was our custom, we walked around the neighbourhood where the house was situated. One whole day I sat on the remains of an old wall in a vacant lot, watching people go in and out. There wasn't a watchman at the corner, luckily enough. The only danger, perhaps, was the silence of that block. The heat was such that I had to take off my shirt: nobody said anything to me, because sweating makes people absent-minded.

The night we had been waiting for finally came. I had to go into the house first, because I was familiar with it and am the least nervous. Penknife and Lathe stayed outside in the bushes holding an empty sack in which to put the objects we picked up. I was supposed to let them know when all was clear for them to come in by hissing like an owl. That night we ate like pigs, with red wine and brandy at the end. The party cost us a bundle.

After some arguments about what time would be best to go into Anibal Celino's house, consulting our watches every fifteen minutes, we walked down Canning Street and stopped in front of the garden of our house, as if we were lost. All of a sudden Penknife and Lathe jumped over the garden fence and hid behind the bushes. I took refuge in the darkness of the entrance to the house, with the picklock in my hand. The shiny face of the lion biting on the ring distracted me for a moment from my task; the door suddenly opened. I jumped back and hid in the plants, but the door remained open. For the longest time a clock struck the hour with a great variety of chimes, then quarter-past, then half-past. I waited for something to happen, scratching my ankle on some confounded branch. Nothing happened; silence succeeded silence, sealing my eyes with sleep, while ants climbed up my legs to my navel. I waited for another fifteen minutes and then went up to the door, which still stood open. I entered the house and turned on the flashlight. I spun the little circle of light around me and then pointed it toward the staircase: sitting on one of the steps was Aurora. I think it was the first time in my life that I was frightened: she looked like a real dwarf because she was wearing a long nightgown and her hair was gathered on top of her head. As if she were waiting for me, she came up to me and whispered in my ear:

"You are the Lord. I have been waiting for you a long time."

I began trembling and whispered: "Who are you waiting for?"

Then, as if she had not listened to what I said, she told me, while waving one of her legs the way a cat does when cleaning its face: "Clotilde Ifran is waiting for me."

"Who is Clotilde Ifran? Where is she?"

"She's in heaven. She's a seer who read my palm. When she died she lay in a beautiful bed, in her shop. She sold corsets. She made girdles and brassieres for ladies and her room had drawers full of pink and blue ribbons, elastic and snaps, buttons and lace. When I went to her house with Mommy and had to wait, she let me play with everything. Sometimes, when I was not in school, and Mommy was off at the theatre or God knows where, she would leave me at Clotilde Ifran's house, so that she could take care of me. That's when I really had fun. She didn't just give me candies or let me play with her needles and scissors and ribbons; she also read my palm or the cards. One day, lying on her bed, pale as a ghost, she said to me: "The Lord will come to get me, and then He will come for you: then we'll be together in heaven." "And will we have as much fun there as we do here?" I asked her. "Much more," she answered, "because the Lord is very good." "And when will He come to get me?" "I don't know when or how, but I'll read the cards to find out," she answered. The next day, huge black horses took her to the Chacarita in a coach covered with black decorations and flowers, and I never saw her again, not even in my dreams. You are the Lord she spoke to me about, for whom there are no closed doors. You wanted to test my loyalty, didn't you, when you came here with that package from the Firpo Drugstore? You are the Lord, because you have a beard."

"I must be, since you say so."

"A Lord, to whom we must give all that we have."

"We'll take beautiful, shiny things, right?"

"We'll put everything in a picnic basket. Wait for me."

Aurora returned with the basket. We went into the living room. Aurora climbed up on a chair and took down a little key from the top of a cabinet. She opened the glass cabinet and started taking out objects to show me. When the basket was full, she closed the cabinet with the key.

"That's it," Aurora said.

At that moment Aurora raised her voice. I told her fearfully: "Be careful. Don't make any noise."

"Mommy takes sleeping pills and not even thunder could wake up Daddy. Do you want me to read the cards? I'll do for you what Clotilde Ifran did for me. Do you want to?"

She hopped down the stairs and brought a deck of cards; then she sat down on one of the steps.

"This is how Clotilde Ifran read the cards."

Aurora shuffled the cards, then dealt them in a row, one by one, on three of the stairs. The movement of her hands back and forth started making me dizzy. (I was afraid of falling asleep: that's the danger of my calm nature.) I proposed that we go to the living room, thinking about the objects I had to pick up there, but she didn't listen to me; with her authoritarian tone, she began teaching me the meaning of the cards.

"This king of spades, with a very serious face, is an enemy of yours. He's waiting for you outside; they're going to kill you. This jack of spades is also waiting for you. Can't you hear the noise in the street? Can't you hear the steps of someone approaching? It's hard to hide at night. At night every sound can be heard and the moonlight is like the light of your conscience. And the plants. Do you think plants can help you? They're our enemies, sometimes, when the police arrive with their weapons drawn. That's why Clotilde Ifran wanted to take me with her. There are so many dangers."

I wanted to leave, but a lethargy like what I feel after having eaten held me back. What would Lathe, the leader, think? Like a drunkard, I went to the door and half-opened it. Someone fired; I fell to the floor like a dead man and lost consciousness.

Report on Heaven and Hell

Following the example of the great auction houses, Heaven and Hell have galleries full of objects that will surprise no one since they are the same things that tend to fill the houses in the world. But it is not enough to speak only of objects: in those halls there are also cities, towns, gardens, mountains, valleys, suns, moons, winds, seas, stars, reflections, temperatures, flavours, perfumes, sounds, for eternity gives us all sorts of feelings and shows.

If, for you, the wind roars like a tiger, or the angelic dove, when it looks at you, has the eyes of a hyena; if the well-dressed man who is crossing the street is dressed in suggestive rags; if the prize-winning rose they give you is but a faded rag, less interesting than a sparrow; if your wife's face is an angry bare stick: your eyes, not God, made them that way.

When you die, the demons and the angels, who are equally eager, knowing that you are sleepy, partly in this world and partly in some other, will come in disguise to your bed and, stroking your head, will ask you to choose the things you preferred in the course of your life. First, in a sort of sample book, they will show you the simple things. If they show you the sun, the moon, or the stars, you will see them in a ball of painted crystal, and you will think this crystal ball is the world;

133

if they show you the sea or the mountains, you will see them in a stone and you will think that stone is the sea or the mountains; if they show you a horse, it will be a miniature, but you will think that horse is a real one. The angels and the demons will confuse your spirit with pictures of flowers, of glazed fruit, of candies; making you think you are still a child, they will sit you in a chair they make of their hands, called the queen's chair or the golden seat, and in that fashion they will carry you, their hands clasped, through those hallways to the centre of your life, where your favourite things are hidden. Be careful. If you choose more things from Hell than from Heaven, you may go to Heaven; on the other hand, if you choose more things from Heaven than from Hell, you run the risk of going to Hell, since your love of celestial things is a sign of mere greed.

The laws of Heaven and Hell are flexible. Whether you go to one place or the other depends on the slightest detail. I know people who—because of a broken key or a wicker bird cage—went to Hell, and others who—for a sheet of newspaper or a glass of milk—went to Heaven.

The Mortal Sin

The symbols of purity and mysticism are at times more aphrodisiac than pornographic pictures or stories: that is why—oh sacrilegious one!—the days before your first Communion, with the promise of a white dress decorated with lots of lace, of linen gloves, and of a rosary of little pearls, were perhaps the most impure days of your life. May God forgive me for it, because in a way I was your accomplice and your slave.

With a red-flowered mimosa, which you picked in the countryside on Sundays, and a missal bound in white (a chalice stamped on the centre of the first page and lists of sins on another), it was then that you discovered the pleasure—as I choose to call it—of love, so as not to call it by its technical name. You would not have been able to give it its technical name either, since you didn't even know where to place it in the list of sins you studied so diligently. Not even in the catechism was everything anticipated or clarified.

When seeing your innocent, melancholy face, nobody suspected that perversity, or rather, vice, already had you caught in its complicated, sticky net.

When some girlfriend arrived to play with you, you would first tell, then show, the secret link between the mimosa flower, the missal, and your inexplicable exhilaration. No friend understood it, or tried to participate in it, but all of them pretended quite the opposite, to oblige you, and they sowed in you that panicky feeling of solitude (which was stronger than you were) of knowing that you were being deceived by your neighbour.

In the enormous house where you lived (from the windows of which you could see more than one church, one store, the river full of ships, sometimes processions of streetcars or carriages in the square, and the English clock), the top floor was devoted to purity and slavery: to the children and the servants. (You were of the opinion that slavery also existed on the other floors and that purity was absent from all of them.)

You heard someone say in a sermon: "Lust is greater, corruption is greater." You wanted to walk barefoot, like the baby Jesus; to sleep in a bed surrounded by animals; to eat bread crumbs, which you would find on the ground, like the birds: but none of these pleasures was granted to you. To console you for not walking barefoot, they dressed you in an iridescent taffeta gown, in shoes of gilded leather; to console you for not sleeping in a bed of straw, they took you to the Colon Theatre, the largest in the world; to console you for not eating crumbs off the ground, they gave you a fancy box of silvery lace paper, full of candies that barely fit in your mouth.

Only rarely that winter did the ladies, with their headgear of feathers and furs, venture into the top floor of the house, whose un-contestable superiority (for you) would attract them in summertime, when they wore light clothes and carried binoculars, in search of a flat roof where they could watch airplanes, an eclipse, or perhaps just the rising of Venus. Then they would pat your head as they went by, exclaiming in falsetto: "What lovely hair! Oh, what lovely hair!"

Next to the room full of toys that also served as the study room was located the men's bathroom, a bathroom you never saw except from afar, through the half-open door. The chief servant, Chango, the one granted most responsibility in the house, who had given you the nickname of Doll, would linger there much longer than the others. You noticed it, because you would often cross the hall to go to the ironing room, a place you found pleasant. From there, you could not only see the shameful entrance: you could hear the sound of the plumbing descending to the countless bedrooms and living rooms in the house, rooms where there were glass cabinets, a small altar with images of the Virgin, and the glow of sunset on the ceiling.

In the elevator, when the nursemaid took you to the room full of toys, you often saw Chango entering the forbidden room with a sly expression on his face and a cigarette in his lips, but even more often you would see him alone, distracted, baffled, in different places around the house, standing up, leaning endlessly on the edge of a table, be it a fancy or a plain one (any table, that is, except the marble one in the kitchen or the wrought-iron one decorated with bronze irises in the courtyard). "What's the matter with Chango, why doesn't he come?" Shrill voices could be heard, calling him. He would linger before moving away from the table. Afterwards, when he did come, no one of course could remember why they had been calling him.

You would spy on him, but he also ended up spying on you: you discovered that the day the mimosa flower disappeared from your desk, a flower that later adorned the buttonhole of his lustrine jacket.

The ladies of the house rarely left you alone, but when there were parties or deaths (and they were very much alike) they would have Chango take care of you. Parties and deaths served to strengthen this custom, apparently preferred by your parents. "Chango is serious. Chango is good. He's better than a governess," they would say in chorus. "Of course, he has fun with her," they would add. But I know of one person with the mouth of a viper, the kind that's never lacking, who said: "A man is a man, but these people don't care at all, so long as they can save a little money." "How unfair!" the raucous aunts would mutter. "The little girl's parents are generous, so generous they pay Chango as if he were a governess."

Someone died, I can't remember who. That intense smell of flowers rose through the elevator shaft, using up and degrading the air. Death, with its countless shows of ostentation, filled the lower floors, went up and down with the elevators, with crosses, coffins, wreaths, palm fronds, and music stands. Upstairs, under Chango's vigilance, you ate chocolates that he gave you; you played with the blackboard, the store, the train, and the doll house. Swift as the dream of a lightning bolt, your mother visited you and asked Chango if there was any need to invite some little girl to play with you. Chango answered that it was better not to, because two of them would make a commotion. A purple colour passed over his cheeks. Your mother gave you a kiss and left; she smiled, showing her beautiful teeth, momentarily happy to see you acting so sensibly in Chango's company.

That day Chango's face was even blurrier than usual: we would not have recognized him in the street, neither you nor I, although you described him to me so many times. You spied on him out of the corner of your eye; he, who usually stood up straight, was curving over like a parenthesis; then he would come up to the corner of the table and stare at you. From time to time he watched the movements of the elevator: inside the black metal cage he could see the cables going by like snakes. You were playing, feeling a submissive uneasiness. You could foresee that something unusual had happened or was going to happen in the house. Like a dog, you could smell the awful scent of flowers. The door was open: it was so tall that its opening was the size of three doors of a modern building, but that would not make your escape any easier; besides, you had no intention of escaping. A mouse or a frog does not flee the snake that desires them; larger animals do not flee either. Chango, dragging his feet, finally moved away from the table; he leaned over the railing on the stairs so as to look down. A woman's voice, shrill and cold, echoed from the basement: "Is Doll behaving properly?"

The echo, so seductive when you spoke to it, repeated the phrase without any sort of enchantment.

"She's behaving wonderfully," Chango answered, hearing his words resound in the lower depths of the basement.

"At five o'clock I will bring her her milk."

Chango's reply, "Don't worry, I'll prepare it for her myself," mixed with a feminine "thank you" and was lost in the tiles of the lower floors.

Chango came back into the room and ordered you: "Look through the keyhole while I'm in the little room next door. I'm going to show you something very beautiful."

He stooped down next to the door and put his eye to the keyhole, to show you how you had to do it. He left the room and you were alone. You kept on playing as if God were watching you, as if you had taken a vow, with that deceptive zeal that children sometimes have when they play. Then, without a moment's hesitation, you went up to the door. You did not need to stoop: the keyhole was right at the height of your eyes. What headless women would you discover? The opening of the keyhole acts as a lens on the image that is seen: the tiles sparkled, a corner of the white wall was brightly lit. Nothing else. A slight draught made your hair blow around and forced you to close your eyes. You moved away from the keyhole, but Chango's voice resounded with a commanding and sweet obscenity: "Doll, look, look." You looked again. Bestial breathing could be felt through the door, no longer just the air from a window open in the adjoining room. I feel such sorrow when I think how horror imitates beauty. Like you and Chango, through that door, Pyramis and Thisbe talked lovingly through a wall.

You drew away from the door again and went automatically back to your games. Chango came back to the room and asked you: "Did you see?" You shook your head, and your straight hair flew around madly. "Did you like it?" Chango insisted, knowing that you were lying. You didn't answer. With a comb you pulled off your doll's wig, but once again Chango was leaning on the edge of the table where you were trying to play. With his troubled look he was staring at the inches that separated the two of you, and almost imperceptibly he slid over next to you. You threw yourself on the floor, holding the doll's ribbon in your hand. You did not move. A series of flushes of red covered your face, like those thin layers of gold that cover fake jewellery. You remembered how Chango had rummaged around in the white underwear in your mother's drawer when he replaced the women servants in the housework. The veins of his hands were all swelled up, as if full of blue ink. On his fingertips you saw he had bruises. Without meaning to, you looked carefully at his lustrine jacket, which felt very rough where it touched your knees. From that moment on, you would always see the tragedies of your life adorned with tiny details. You missed the neat flower of the mimosa, your misunderstood sickness, but you felt that this arcane spectacle, brought about by unforeseen circumstances, must needs accomplish its goal: the impossible violation of your solitude. Like two very similar criminals, you and Chango were united by different objects, but were pointed toward identical goals.

During sleepless nights you composed dishonest reports that would serve as confessions of your guilt. Your first Communion arrived. You could not find a modest or clear or concise form of confession. You had to take Communion in a state of mortal sin. In the pews were not only the members of your family, which was large, but

also Chango and Camila Figueira, Valeria Ramos, Celina Eyzaguirre
and Romagnoli, the priest from another parish. With the sorrow of a
parricide, of someone condemned to death for treason, you entered
the church as if frozen, biting on the corner of your missal. I see you
pale, not blushing before the high altar, with your linen gloves on,
holding a bouquet of artificial flowers, like a bride's bouquet, by your
waist. I would wander on foot across the whole world to search for you
like a missionary to save you if only you had the luck, which you don't
have, of being my contemporary. I know that for a long time, in the
darkness of your room, you heard, with that insistence that silence
reveals on the cruel lips of the furies who devote themselves to
tormenting children, the inhuman voices, linked to your own voice,
saying: it is a mortal sin, my God, it is a mortal sin.

How were you able to survive? Only a miracle can explain it: the
miracle of mercy.

The Expiation

for Helena and Eduardo

Antonio summoned Ruperto and me to the room at the back of the house. With a domineering tone he ordered us to sit down. The bed was made. He went into the patio to open the door of the aviary, then came back and lay down on the bed.

"I'm going to show you a demonstration," he told us.

"Are they going to hire you in a circus?" I asked him.

He whistled two or three times and Favorita, Maria Callas, and Mandarin, the little red one, flew in. Staring hard at the ceiling, he whistled once more in a still higher, more tremulous tone. Was that the demonstration? Was that why he had called Ruperto and me? Why didn't he wait for Cleobula to arrive? I thought that the whole performance was meant to show that Ruperto was not blind but crazy; that he would reveal his madness through some show of emotion when he witnessed Antonio's feat. The canaries' flight back and forth made me sleepy. My memories flew around my mind with equal persistence. They say that you relive your life the moment before your death: I relived mine that afternoon with an aloof feeling of distress.

As if it were painted on the wall, I saw my marriage to Antonio at five o'clock

141

one December afternoon. It was quite hot and, when we got home, with some
surprise, I noticed a canary from the window of the bedroom where I was taking
off my wedding dress and my veil. Now I realize that it was this same
Mandarin who was pecking on the last orange on the tree in the courtyard.
Antonio did not interrupt his kisses when he saw me so interested in that spec-
tacle. The bird's extreme cruelty to the orange fascinated me. I watched the scene
until Antonio dragged me trembling to the marriage bed, whose bedspread,
lying among the wedding presents, had been a source of happiness for him and
of terror for me during the days before the wedding. The bedspread of scarlet-
coloured velvet was embroidered with a journey in a stagecoach. I closed my
eyes and was barely conscious of what happened next. Love is also a journey;
for a period of many days I gradually learned its lessons, without seeing or
understanding the pleasure or pain it lavished on one. At first, I think Antonio
and I loved each other equally, without any problems, except for those caused
by my innocence and his shyness.

This tiny house is located with its equally tiny garden at the edge of
town. The healthy air of the mountains surrounds us: the countryside
is nearby and we can see it when we open the windows.

We already had a radio and a refrigerator. Numerous friends filled our
house on holidays or to celebrate some family occasion. What else could we hope
for? Cleobula and Ruperto visited us even more frequently because they were
our childhood friends. Antonio had fallen in love with me; they knew about it.
He had not sought me out or chosen me; rather, I was the one who had chosen
him. His only ambition in life was to be loved by his wife, that she should
preserve her fidelity. He gave little importance to money.

Ruperto would sit down in a corner of the patio and, as he tuned his guitar,
would abruptly ask for a mate, or, if it was hot, for a lemonade. I thought of him
as one of the various friends or relatives who form part, one might say, of the
furniture of a house, noticed only when broken or located in a different place
than usual.

"The canaries are born singers," Cleobula would invariably say, but
if she could have, she would have killed them with a broom, for she
detested them. What would she have said if she had seen them do all
those ridiculous demonstrations without Antonio even offering them
a piece of lettuce or a vanilla wafer!

I would give Ruperto the mate or the glass of lemonade, mechanically, in the
shade of the arbour where he always sat in a Viennese chair, like a dog always
in its place. I didn't think of him as a woman thinks of a man; I didn't behave

with the slightest flirtation in my dealings with him. Many times, after washing my hair, with my wet hair put up with hairpins, looking like a fright, or with my toothbrush in my mouth and toothpaste on my lips, or with my hands covered with soap suds from washing the clothes, with my apron fastened at the waist, big-bellied as if I were pregnant, I would let him in, opening the front door for him without even looking at him. Many times, such was my negligence that I think he saw me leaving the bathroom wrapped in a Turkish towel, dragging my slippers like an old woman or any woman whatsoever.

Chusco, Albahaca and Serranito flew to the bowl that held little arrows made of thorns. Carrying the arrows they eagerly flew to other bowls containing a dark liquid in which they moistened the tiny arrowheads. They looked like toy birds, cheap toothpick holders, decorations for great-great-grandmother's hat.

Cleobula, who is not overly suspicious, had noticed that Ruperto looked at me too insistently, and told me about it. "What eyes he has," she would repeat endlessly, "what eyes!"

"I have succeeded in keeping my eyes open when I sleep," Antonio mumbled; "that is one of the most difficult tests I have set myself in my life."

I was startled by his voice. Was that the demonstration? After all, what was so extraordinary about that?

"Like Ruperto," I said with a strange voice.

"Like Ruperto," Antonio repeated. "The canaries obey my orders more easily than my eyelids."

The three of us were in that dark room as if doing penance. But— what connection could there be between his eyes being open when he slept and the orders he gave the canaries? Not surprisingly, Antonio left me rather perplexed: he was so different from other men!

Cleobula had also assured me that while Ruperto tuned the guitar he would stare at me from the top of my head to the tips of my toes, and that one night when he fell asleep, half-drunk, in the patio, his eyes had fixed on me. In consequence, I lost my naturalness with him, and perhaps my lack of flirtation. To my way of thinking, Ruperto looked at me through a kind of mask in which his animal eyes were mounted, those eyes that didn't close even when he was sleeping. His pupils would pierce me, fixing on me in a mysterious way, with God knows what in mind, as he would look at the glass of lemonade or the mate that I would serve him. Eyes that looked so hard did not exist in the whole province, in the whole world; a deep-blue gleam, as if the sky were inside them, made them different from all others, from looks that seemed listless or dead. Ruperto was not a man: he was a pair of eyes, without a face or voice or body; that's how I saw him, though Antonio saw him differently. For days on end he would become annoyed by my inattention, and for the slightest trifle he would speak harshly to me or force me to do unpleasant tasks, as if instead of his wife I were his slave. The transformation in Antonio's character upset me.

How strange men are! What was the demonstration he wanted to show us? The business about the circus was no joke.

Shortly after we got married, he would often leave his job, under the pretext of a headache or an inexplicable pain in the gut. Are all husbands alike?

At the back of the house there was a huge aviary full of canaries; formerly Antonio had always taken care of it zealously, but now it was neglected. In the morning, when I had time, I would clean the aviary, putting birdseed, water, and lettuce in the white bowls and, when the females were about to lay their eggs, would help them prepare the little nests. Antonio had always busied himself with these things, but he no longer showed any interest in doing so nor in my doing it.

We'd been married for two years! And no children! On the other hand, how many young the canaries had borne!

An aroma of musk and cedron filled the room. The canaries smelled like chickens, Antonio smelled of tobacco and sweat, but Ruperto lately smelled of nothing but alcohol. They told me he got drunk. How dirty the room was! Birdseed, bread crumbs, lettuce leaves, cigarette butts and ashes covered the floor.

Since childhood, Antonio had devoted his spare time to taming animals. He first used his art, for he was a true artist, on a dog, then on a horse, then on a skunk that had had its glands removed, which he carried for a time in his pocket; later, when he met me, he decided to tame canaries, because I liked them. During the months of our engagement, to win me over, he had sent them to me bearing slips of paper with expressions of love on them, or flowers tied with a little ribbon. From his house to mine there were fifteen long blocks: the winged messengers went from one house to the other without hesitation. Believe it or not, they would even put the flowers in my hair or the slips of paper in the pocket of my blouse.

Wasn't it more difficult for the canaries to put flowers in my hair or slips of paper in my pockets than to do the silly things they were doing with the confounded arrows?

In town, Antonio came to enjoy a great deal of prestige. "If you hypnotize women as you do birds, no one will resist your charms," his aunts told him, with the hope that their nephew would marry some millionairess. As I said before, Antonio was not interested in money. From the age of fifteen on, he worked as a mechanic, earning as much as he wanted, which was what he offered me in marriage. We lacked nothing for our happiness. I could not understand why Antonio did not find some pretext to make Ruperto go away. Any motive would have sufficed, even a quarrel because of a job or politics, something which, without coming to blows or arms, would have prevented that friend of his from coming to our house. Antonio did not let any of his feelings show, except in the form of a change of character I knew how to interpret. Despite my usual modesty, I noticed that the jealousy I inspired drove a man I had always considered a model of normal behaviour nearly out of his mind.

Antonio whistled, took off his shirt. His naked torso looked as if it were of bronze. I trembled when I saw him. I remember that before marrying him I had blushed before a statue that greatly resembled him. But hadn't I seen him naked? Why did he so surprise me?

But Antonio's character underwent another change that reassured me in part: his laziness turned into extreme activity, his melancholy into apparent happiness. His life became filled with mysterious occupations, with goings and comings that signified an extreme interest in life. After supper, we no longer had even a moment of rest to listen to the radio or read the paper, or to do nothing, or to chat for a few minutes about the events of the day. Sundays and holidays also were no longer a pretext for giving ourselves a rest. I, who am a mirror of Antonio, was infected with his restlessness, and came and went through the house, putting closets in order that were already in order, or washing pristine pillow cases, from an irresistible need to take part in my husband's enigmatic activities. A redoubled love and interest in the birds occupied him for much of the day. He set up new props in the aviary; the dry branch, in the middle, was replaced by another larger and more graceful one, that made the aviary more beautiful.

Dropping their arrows, two canaries started fighting; their feathers flew around the room, and Antonio's face grew dark with rage. Was he capable of killing them? Cleobula had told me he was cruel. "He looks like someone who carries a knife in his belt," she explained.

Antonio no longer allowed me to clean the aviary. During that period, he occupied a room that served as a storage room at the back of the house, leaving our marriage bed. On a cot, where my brother used to nap when he visited,

Antonio spent his nights (without sleeping, I suspect, since I would hear his tireless paces on the flagstones until dawn). Sometimes he would shut himself up for hours at a time in that damned room.

One by one, the canaries let the little arrows fall from their beaks, perched on the back of a chair, and sang a soft song. Antonio sat up and, looking at Maria Callas, the one he had always called "the queen of disobedience," said a word that meant nothing to me. The canaries began fluttering about.

Through the painted glass of the window panes I tried to observe his movements. Once I intentionally cut my hand with a knife so as to be able to knock on his door. When he opened it, a flock of canaries came flying out, returning to the aviary. Antonio cured my wound but, as if he suspected it was a pretext to get his attention, treated me with coolness and suspicion. It was about that time that he went away for two weeks, in a truck, I don't know where, and came back with a sack full of plants.

I looked at my stained skirt out of the corner of my eye. Birds are so tiny and so dirty. Exactly when had they soiled me? I looked at them with hatred: I like to be clean even in the darkness of a room.

Ruperto, ignorant of the bad impression his visits were making, came with the same frequency and always with the same habits. Sometimes, when I left the patio to avoid his glances, my husband would find some pretext to make me return. I thought that somehow he enjoyed what gave him such displeasure. Ruperto's glances now seemed obscene to me; they stripped me naked in the shadow of the arbour, forced me to do unspeakable acts when a late afternoon breeze caressed my cheeks. Antonio, on the other hand, never looked at me, or pretended never to look at me, according to Cleobula. One of my most burning desires at that time was not to have ever met him, not to have married him, not to have known his caresses, but to meet him anew, discover him, give myself to him. But who can recover what has already been lost?

I sat up; my legs hurt. I don't like being still for such a long time. How I envy the birds who can fly! But canaries make me sad. They look like they suffer when they obey.

Antonio did not try to avoid Ruperto's visits: on the contrary, he encouraged them. During Carnival, he went to the extreme of inviting him to stay at our house, one night when he stayed especially late. We had to put him up in the room that Antonio was occupying for the moment. That night, as if it were the most natural thing in the world, we slept together again, my husband and I, in the marriage bed. My life returned to its old pattern at that moment; at least that's what I thought.

I glimpsed the famous doll in a corner, under the night table. I thought of picking it up. As if I had made some gesture, Antonio told me: "Don't move."

I remembered the day during Carnival week when, while straightening up the bedrooms, I discovered that burlap doll in the top of Antonio's closet, as punishment for my sins: its large blue eyes of some soft material like fabric, with two dark circles in the middle representing the pupils. Dressed as a gaucho it would have served to decorate our bedroom. Laughing, I showed it to Antonio, who looked annoyed and pulled it out of my hands.

"It's a memento of my childhood," he told me. "I don't like you touching my things."

"What's wrong with touching a doll you played with when you were a boy? I know boys who play with dolls—does it make you ashamed? Aren't you a man by now?" I said.

"I don't have to explain anything. You'd better shut up."

In a foul mood, Antonio once again stored the doll in the top of the closet and didn't speak to me for several days. But we hugged one another tight as in happier days past.

I touched my damp forehead with my hand. Had my curls come undone? Luckily there wasn't a mirror in the room, otherwise I wouldn't have resisted the temptation to look at myself instead of looking at those stupid canaries.

Antonio frequently shut himself up in the back room, and I noticed that he would leave open the door of the aviary so that some of the birds could come in the window. Moved by curiosity, one afternoon I spied on him, standing on a chair, since the window was very high (which of course prevented me from looking into the room when I passed through the courtyard).

I saw Antonio's naked torso. Was it my husband or a statue? He accused Ruperto of being crazy, but he was perhaps even crazier himself. How much money he had spent on canaries, instead of buying me a washing machine!

One day I caught a glimpse of the doll lying on the bed. A swarm of birds surrounded it. The room had been turned into a kind of laboratory. One clay bowl held a bunch of leaves, stems, and dark pieces of bark; another, some little arrows made of thorns; another, a shiny brown liquid. It seemed to me I had seen those objects in my dreams. To overcome my anxiety I described the scene to Cleobula, who answered: "That's what the Indians do: they use arrows with curare."

I didn't ask her what curare was. I didn't know whether she was telling me this with scorn or admiration.

"They devote themselves to sorcery. Your husband is an Indian." When she saw my surprise, she asked: "Didn't you know that?"

I shook my head with irritation. My husband was my husband. I had never thought that he could belong to a race or world different from my own.

"How do you know?" I asked with some vehemence.

"Haven't you looked at his eyes, his protruding cheek-bones? Haven't you noticed how cunning he is? Mandarin, even Mariá Callas, are more frank than he is. That reserve, that way of not answering when you ask him something, that way of treating women: aren't they enough to show you he's an Indian? My mother knows all about it. They took him from a reservation when he was five years old. Perhaps that's what you liked about him: that mystery that makes him different from other men."

Antonio was perspiring and the sweat made his torso shine. He was so handsome and yet how he wasted time! Had I married Juan Leston, the lawyer, or Roberto Cuentas, the bookseller, I surely would not have suffered so much. But—what sensitive woman marries from self-interest? They say that there are men who train fleas, and what good is that?

I lost confidence in Cleobula. No doubt she was telling me that my husband was an Indian to upset me or make me lose confidence in him; but one day, while looking through a history book that had illustrations of Indian camps, and Indians on horseback swinging boleadoras, *I noticed a similarity between Antonio and those naked men adorned with feathers. At the same time I noticed that what had attracted me to Antonio may have been the difference between him and my brothers and their friends, the bronze colour of his skin, his slanted eyes, and that cunning air Cleobula had mentioned with perverse delight.*

"And the demonstration?" I asked.

Antonio did not answer me. He looked fixedly at the canaries, which had started fluttering again. Mandarin separated himself from his fellows and remained alone in the darkness, singing a song similar to that of a lark.

My solitude was increasing. I had nobody to tell of my worries.

For Holy Week, for the second time, Antonio insisted that Ruperto stay as a guest in our house. It rained, as it always tends to rain for Holy Week. We went to church with Cleobula for the Stations of the Cross.

"How is the Indian?" Cleobula asked me rudely.

"Who?"

"The Indian, your husband," she answered. "In town everyone calls him that."

"I like Indians, and even if my husband were not one of them, I would still like them," I answered, trying not to interrupt my prayers.

Antonio stood as if in prayer. Had he ever prayed? On our wedding day my mother had asked him to take Communion; Antonio refused to accommodate her.

In the meanwhile Antonio's friendship with Ruperto was becoming closer. A sort of camaraderie, from which I was in some way excluded, linked them in a way that seemed right to me. At that time Antonio made a show of his powers. To amuse himself, he sent messages to Ruperto, at home in his house, via the canaries. People said they played truco *in this way, since they once exchanged Tarot cards. Were they making fun of me? I felt upset by the games of those two grown-up men and decided not to take them seriously. Did I have to admit that friendship was more important than love? Nothing had estranged Antonio and Ruperto; on the other hand Antonio, to some extent unfairly, had become estranged from me. With my woman's pride, I suffered. Ruperto kept on looking at me. The whole drama: was it just a farce? Did I miss the conjugal drama, that torture inflicted on me by the jealousy of a husband who had gone mad for days at a time?*

We continued to love each other, in spite of everything.

In the circus Antonio could earn some money with his demonstrations, so why not? Maria Callas nodded her head to one side, then to the other, and perched on the back of a chair.

One morning, as if he were announcing that a house was burning down, Antonio entered my room and said to me: "Ruperto is dying. They called me to come. I am going to see him."

I waited for Antonio until noon, distracted by the housework. He returned when I was washing my hair.

"Let's go," he told me. "Ruperto is in the courtyard. I saved him."

"How? Was it a joke?"

"No, not at all. I saved him by means of artificial respiration."

Hurriedly, without understanding anything, I put up my hair, got dressed, and went out to the yard. Ruperto, motionless, was standing by the door, looking at the flagstones of the courtyard without seeing them. Antonio pulled up a chair so that Ruperto could sit down.

Antonio didn't look at me; he stared at the roof, as if holding his breath. Suddenly Mandarin flew by Antonio and stuck one of the arrows in his arm. I applauded: I thought that's what I should do to make Antonio happy. It was nonetheless an absurd demonstration. Why didn't he use his gift to cure Ruperto?

That fatal day, when Ruperto sat down, he covered his face with his hands. How much he had changed! I looked at his cold, inert face, his dark hands.

When would they leave me alone? I had to put the curlers in my wet hair. I asked Ruperto, hiding my annoyance: "What's happened?"

A long silence trembled in the sun, making the song of the birds stand out. Ruperto finally answered: "I dreamed that the canaries were pecking on my arms, my neck, my chest; that I couldn't close my eyelids to protect my eyes. I dreamed that my legs and arms were as heavy as bags of sand. My hands could not scare off those monstrous beaks that were pecking on my pupils. I slept without sleeping, as if I had taken some drug. When I awoke from that dream, which was no dream at all, I saw darkness; nevertheless, I could hear the birds sing and the normal sounds of morning. With a great effort I called my sister, who came over. With a voice that was not my own, I told her: 'You must call Antonio to come save me.' 'From what?' my sister asked. I couldn't utter another word. My sister went running out, and came back with Antonio half an hour later. A half-hour that seemed like an eternity to me! Slowly, as Antonio moved my arms back and forth, I regained my strength but not my eyesight."

"I'm going to make a confession to you," Antonio whispered, and he slowly added, "but without words."

Favorita followed Mandarin and stuck an arrow in Antonio's neck, then Maria Callas flew over his chest for a moment, sticking in another little arrow. Antonio's eyes, fixed on the roof, changed colour, you could say. Was Antonio an Indian? Do Indians have blue eyes? In some way his eyes resembled Ruperto's.

"What's the meaning of all of this?" I mumbled.

"What's he doing?" Ruperto said, since he understood nothing.

Antonio didn't answer. As still as a statue, he received the seemingly harmless arrows that the canaries were sticking in him. I went up to the bed and shook him.

"Answer me," I said. "Answer me. What's the meaning of all of this?"

He did not answer me. Crying, I embraced him, throwing myself on top of his body; losing all shame, I kissed him on the mouth, as only a movie star would do. A swarm of canaries fluttered about my head.

That morning Antonio looked at Ruperto with horror. Now I understood that Antonio was guilty twice over: so that no one would discover his crime, he had said to me and to all the world: "Ruperto has gone crazy. He believes he is blind, but he sees as well as the rest of us."

Just as light had left Ruperto's eyes, so love left our house. You could say that those glances were a necessary part of our love. The gatherings in the courtyard lacked life. Antonio fell into a dark sorrow. He explained to me: "A friend's madness is worse than death. Ruperto can see, but he believes he's blind."

I thought with indignation, perhaps with jealousy, that friendship was more important than love in the life of a man.

When I stopped kissing Antonio and drew my face away from his, I noticed that the canaries were about to peck at his eyes. I covered his face with my face and hair, thick as a blanket. I ordered Ruperto to close the door and windows so the room would become completely dark, hoping the canaries would fall asleep. My legs hurt. How long had I been in that position? I don't know. Then I gradually understood Antonio's confession. It was a confession that bound me to him in a frenzy, in a frenzy of misfortune. I understood the pain he had needed to put up with in order to sacrifice—in such an ingenious way, with that tiny dose of curare and with those winged monsters that obeyed his whimsical commands as if they were orderlies—the eyes of Ruperto, his friend, and his own, so that they, poor things, would never be able to look at me again.

Livio Roca

He was tall, dark, and quiet. I never saw him laugh or hurry for any reason whatsoever. His chestnut eyes never looked at anything straight on. He wore a kerchief tied around his neck and always had a cigarette in his mouth. He was ageless. His name was Livio Roca, but he was called Dumbo because he pretended to be deaf. He was lazy, but in his periods of leisure (he did not think of inactivity as laziness) he fixed watches that he never returned to their owners. Whenever I could, I'd escape to visit Livio Roca. I met him during vacation, one day in January when we went to spend the summer in Cachari. I was nine years old. He was always the poorest member of the family, the most unhappy, according to the relatives. He lived in a house that resembled a railroad car. He loved Clemencia; she was perhaps his only consolation and the main subject of gossip in the town. Her velvet nose, cold ears, curved neck, short, soft hair, and her obedience were all reasons to love her. I understood him. At night, when he unsaddled her, he would take a long time to say goodbye to her, as if the heat of her sweaty body gave him life and took it back from him when he went away. He let her drink so as to prolong the farewell, even if she wasn't thirsty. He hesitated before bringing her into his shack to sleep at night, under cover, in the winter. He hesitated because he feared what would later in fact happen: people said he was crazy, completely crazy. Tonga was the first to say that. Tonga, with his embittered expression and needle-like eyes, dared to criticize him and Clemencia. Neither of them could ever forgive him. I also loved Clemencia in my own way.

In the room full of trunks there was Grandma Indalecia Roca's silk bathrobe. It was a sort of relic that lay at the feet of a Virgin who was painted green and had a broken foot. From time to time, Tonga and the other members of the family, or some visitor, would place unlucky flowers or little bouquets of herbs that smelled like mint there, or sweet, bright-coloured drinks. There were times when a crooked candle of various colours would tremble with a dying flame at the foot of the Virgin; for this reason the bathrobe had large drops of paraffin the size of buttons, which decorated instead of dirtying it. Time eliminated these rituals little by little: the ceremonies happened more and more rarely. Perhaps for this reason, Livio ventured to use the bathrobe to make a hat for Clemencia. (I helped him do so.) I think that's what caused the misunderstanding with the rest of the family. Tonga called him a degenerate, and one of the brothers-in-law, who was a bricklayer, called him a drunkard. Livio put up with these insults without defending himself. The insults started bothering him only some days later.

He couldn't remember his childhood except for the unhappiness. He had scabies for nine months and conjunctivitis for nine more, according to what he told me while we were sewing the hat. Perhaps all of that contributed to his losing faith in any kind of happiness for the rest of his existence. At the age of eighteen, when he met his cousin Malvina and got engaged to her, perhaps he had a foreboding of disaster at the moment he gave her the engagement ring. Instead of becoming happy he was sad. They had grown up together: from the moment he decided to marry her he knew the union would not be a happy one. Malvina's friends, who were numerous, spent their time embroidering sheets and tablecloths and nightgowns for her with her initials on them, but they never used those things, embroidered with such love. Malvina died two days after the wedding. They dressed her as a bride and put her in the coffin with a bouquet of orange blossoms. Poor Livio couldn't look at her, but in the darkness of his hands, where he hid his eyes the night they held a wake for her, he offered her his faithfulness in the form of a gold ring. He never spoke to any other woman, not even to my cousins, who are very ugly; at the shows he didn't look at the actresses. Many times people tried to find a girlfriend for him. They would bring them over in the afternoon and sit them down on the wicker chair: one was blond and wore glasses, and they called her the English girl; another was dark with braids, and a flirt; another, the most serious of them all, was a giant with a pin head. It was hopeless. That's why he loved Clemencia with all his heart, because women didn't count for him. But one night, one of those inevitable uncles with a mocking smile on his lips wanted to punish him for the sacrilege he had committed on grandmother's robe, and shot Clemencia. Mixed with Clemencia's neighing we could hear the murderer's loud laughter.

The Doll

Everybody says: *I am such and such, I am so and so,* except for me, who would prefer not to be who I am. I'm a soothsayer. I suspect at times that I don't merely see the future, but that I provoke it. I began my apprenticeship in Las Ortigas. I have an office in La Magdalena. Clouds of dust, the police, and my clients all pester me.

In accordance with the expert counsel of the doctors, my identity papers declare that I am twenty-nine years old. My mother died the day of my birth, that much they all agree on. They also told me something I prefer to recall now: that someone found me one January night in the pastures by Las Ortigas. Throughout my life, the reports they have given me about my birth have varied widely. I have no reason to believe in some of them more than others. Nevertheless, I prefer to imagine being born in those pastures next to a lagoon surrounded by willows, and not at the door of the shed where they store corn and wool beneath a corrugated iron roof. The lagoon has lots of birds and a bed of white sand; the willows cast trembling shadows that resemble flocks of sheep or the horses that look like Eriberto Soto. The shed is full of cats and sheepskins. At night the cats wail and jump up on the scales. There are fleas, lots of fleas, and red ants.

In one version of my birth, my mother was Polish and wore a new

dress and a pair of black patent-leather shoes; in another, she was
Italian, wore a threadbare dress, and carried a bundle of firewood; in
another, she was just a schoolgirl who carried a notebook and two
books (one for geography and the other for history) under her arm; in
another, she was a filthy gypsy who carried Tarot cards and gold coins
in the pocket of her red skirt. There was even someone who gave me
a fake photograph of my mother. For a time this image excited my
filial sentiments. I put the photograph at the head of my bed and for
days on end would direct my prayers to it. Later, I found out that the
photograph was that of a movie star and that someone had cut it from
an old magazine to make me happy or to torment me. I still preserve
it with a bouquet of dried flowers.

All through my childhood, which seemed very long to me, people
used to tell me the story of my birth to entertain me. Miss Domicia
enlivened her story by drawing cups and houses in a notebook filled
with graph paper. When she took off her glasses to clean them with a
white handkerchief, she would always speak to me of a lagoon where
there were many willows and where birds filled the morning. My
eyelids, the door to sleep, would close. Miss Domicia was methodical.
For the two years I lived with her, before we had the fight which I will
describe later, she would enter and leave my room at the same hour
every day. She would tell me the same story in the same words. On her
belt, she carried a bunch of keys, which fascinated me. Her dark hair
was dry, straight, and long; she always wore it braided and coiled
around either side of her head. Miss Domicia was a sort of head maid,
hated by the other servants. During her tenure, the house was fresh,
clean, orderly; so she was assured by Mr Ildefonso, who was a little
afraid of her. The sets of sheets edged with hemstitches according to
her instructions were never mixed, as they had been in other periods,
with the embroidered tablecloths and the napkins. The bedspreads
were not torn or stained with coffee or rust. Miss Domicia was the
guardian angel of the cupboards, of the pantry. With a ringing of keys,
she would open the huge doors of the cabinets where soap, jam, wine,
dried fruit, tea, coffee, cookies, and sweets were kept, and those which
held white clothes covered with lace and embroidery and edged with
hems.

Miss Domicia was not fond of me: she would wash my hands with
boiling water; she would twist my toes when she put on my socks;

when she rubbed my face with a handkerchief, she would squash my nose so hard that tears would well up. If I mention her first of all, it is because she was the one who discovered my gift of second sight. As if it were today, I remember a rainy day in January. We were not allowed to go out to the covered yard to play. From the living-room windows we watched the branches of the trees whipped by the wind. Suddenly, in the midst of my games, I announced the arrival of Kaminsky the engineer.

Mr Kaminsky had visited the ranch only once. His name and his height had made a vivid impression on me. With a careful pantomime I described his arrival, which occurred several hours later. Miss Domicia, with her hard, dry hands, pulled the damp hair from my forehead, looked at my eyes with her spiderlike eyes, and told me: "You scoundrel, you must be a witch." What was a witch? I guessed that she must be saying something awful to me. I suddenly pulled her hands away from my forehead. She insisted on brushing my hair, even as I struggled, kicking and screaming, to avoid the touch of her hands. How long did the fight last? I don't know. It seemed to me that it filled, that it would fill up, the whole of my life. We ended up shut in the bathroom. I had been hurt. Miss Domicia wet my head and eyelids with cold water and punished me. She promised never to touch me again, a promise she kept most strictly. On numerous occasions she said that it would have been better for everyone had the old woman at Las Rosas taken care of me. She also said that my presence at the ranch bothered the adults and perverted the children. I tried not to hear her words or look at her face, a face that seemed to me to incarnate that of the devil. By mistake, a shameful mistake in my opinion, and going against all the teachings I had been given, I imagined the devil as belonging to the female and not the male sex (as his dress indicated in the illustrations where I had seen him, in which he looked like a bat, with a black cape in the form of wings).

The old Las Rosas woman—that's how they called Lucia Almeira because she lived at the cattle station at Las Rosas—took me in, as they told me, the night I was born, and kept me in her house until I was three years old. Perhaps I'm confusing my memories with the stories I was forced to listen to. I don't know. A room with a dirt floor: a sheep dog and five chickens with their chicks were lodged with me at Lucia

Almeira's house.

Lucia was thin, wrinkled and dark. I never saw her sitting down. She was always moving from one side of the room to the other. She was so poor that her shoes had no soles. Why had she taken me in? How did she feed me? No one ever knew. Some people said that she planned to raise me to make me work in the circus in town; others said that she loved children madly and that by taking me in she was realizing one of her dreams. In her hands, wrinkled and black, I remember the bits of bread she gave me; I also remember the straw mat with which she covered the window opening to help me sleep and the flatness of her chest where I could hear the beating of her heart.

Those silent days, days in which my memory barely glimpses a few tiny details of the world around me, Lucia Almeira took jealous care of me; all of the stories coincide in that fact. She took me to the Rivas household three times a week when she went to do the washing. While she washed, I would play with torn old rags, with pine cones, with cats (until one of them gave me an unpleasant scratch). Playing with the children in the house, I learned to walk. They got so used to seeing me that at nightfall, when Lucia said goodbye and picked me up to take me home, some of them would cry.

Lucia Almeira consented to my spending one night, Christmas night, in the Rivas house. She allowed me to do so again on later occasions when the children at the ranch begged her. Little by little she got used to what had once seemed impossible for her: being separated from me. Perhaps the illness that was later to cause her death had weakened her to the point where it took away her desire to keep me and take care of me as if I were her daughter. Perhaps Esperanza's enthusiasm for me made her jealous. On one occasion, she didn't come to get me. After a long consultation, Mr Ildefonso convinced her it was better to let me stay on forever at the ranch.

Esperanza liked my company. Mr Ildefonso thought my stay at the house would make his daughter forget the puppy from which she never parted. Instead of playing with the dog, Esperanza would play with me.

Esperanza forgot the dog, and I forgot Lucia.

I don't remember when I came to that yellow house. I feel as if I've always known it. Esperanza showed me its most secret corners: the attic and the mouse room, which is what we called a sort of dark cell where empty bottles and sacks were piled. The house had an enclosed courtyard and a cistern, a corridor with blue flagstones, and Gothic arches over the front door, which was decorated with panes whose white designs looked like lace work. The trees that surrounded it, almost all of them eucalyptus and Australian pines, were very tall and very tangled.

Esperanza and I were the same height and the same age. When we ran races she always beat me, because she managed to cheat in some quick, skillful way. When we climbed trees she would insist that the highest branch I reached was much lower than hers, even when mine was much higher than hers.

Esperanza's arms were covered with freckles. She was cheerful and quick; when she shouted, the veins in her neck would stand out and she would turn very red. She liked scratching. The marks of her fingernails were etched in my skin with purple lines that would last for days. Many times I thought she belonged to the feline family, and that that was why her favourite dog was so overjoyed when it was free of her. I could never love her. I liked boys and, no matter how boorish and unpleasant they were, they seemed superior to girls to me.

My bedroom was located in the wing of the house that faced forward. I slept with a nursemaid who would wake me up to ask me if I had said the Our Father, if I was afraid, if I was asleep. She took care of me only at night.

Across from my door, on the other side of the courtyard, was the boys' room. Before they went to bed, to scare us, they would bang on our windowpanes and imitate the cry of the owls. I often cried for fear, while Elsa, the nursemaid, stood before the mirror slathering her face with cold cream and curling her hair around slips of paper. Often I buried my tears in the pillow as I watched her close the shutters, after opening them slightly to peer out.

For me, the stormy nights were the only calm ones. It seemed to me that the house, like Noah's Ark, was floating on water, and that nobody would come to bother the sleep of a crew composed of evil men and good animals. I had forgiven the cat for its scratch, but I did not forgive Esperanza or Miss Domicia for their devious iniquities.

Since the day I had announced Mr Kaminsky's arrival, some people treated me with more respect. Soon I began predicting the weather, announcing early in the morning whether or not letters would arrive that day, whether the rabbits would die. One day when Mr Ildefonso was leaving for market he asked me whether the calves would sell for a good price. Without a moment's hesitation, I gave an answer that later turned out to be the truth.

Mr Ildefonso was stocky, his hair thick and black, and his green eyes would shine with extraordinary brightness; he wore a reddish straw hat, the top of which was full of little holes; he held this hat on with a leather thong under the chin. He spoke in an emphatic way, pronouncing the last syllables of each word as if they were a threat. He always wore a handkerchief knotted around his neck and a tie pin with a little pearl set in gold. Everything about him indicated an orderly, neat, domineering person. I often heard people talking about him in respectful terms, terms much more respectful than those I heard applied to his wife, Celina, whose ill-apportioned acts of charity earned her some of the local people's lasting resentment. Mrs Celina seemed distant to me, like a portrait. Her precarious health forced her to get up late, to go out only briefly with a parasol, to take long naps, and to go to bed early. She always dressed in white, in long skirts, and looked very tall. Sometimes she covered the upper part of her face with a blue veil; on those occasions, her mouth, with its sweet smile, would receive all of my attention. Mrs Celina let me approach her without fear. She always had on grey gloves and took them off only to close her parasol. After closing the parasol, she would straighten her ring so that the blue stone would show, then she would pass her bare hands over her forehead, as if the hands or the forehead were not her own. She would absent-mindedly kiss her children one by one, and me too, not without some feeling of aversion. Horacio, who was always the last one, would merit the longest, quietest kiss. I never knew whether that pause was purposely directed to Horacio or whether it was part of an absent-mindedness that automatically turned the last kiss into the longest one. Motionless, I always watched that kiss, a gesture that remained so deeply engraved on my memory. It seemed to me that a secret form of voluptuousness always presided over such moments: it was a morning of sunshine and ripe fruit, an evening when the grass was covered with dew.

Celina Rosas incarnated all the virtues of sweetness and refinement for me. Her room, where the window blinds were almost always shut, was a sort of altar forbidden to the rest of us mortals. When I passed the sometimes half-open door, I used to glimpse the floral patterns of the curtains and the mysterious bronze bed where she slept. I thought her life was not in contact with that of the others.

Esperanza and I ate in the pantry; Juan Alberto, Luis, and Horacio ate in the dining room. After meals, while they were serving the coffee, we would play cops and robbers, London Bridge, and tag.

During one of those listless periods after dinner, while Mr Ildefonso was smoking his cigar and Mrs Celina was looking absent-mindedly out of the window, with one cheek resting on her hand, a scene revealed the falseness of the calm that ruled over that house.

Mrs Celina's absence did not seem to sadden Horacio. It surprised me that those long kisses in the morning and evening had not left a greater mark on his heart. Horacio, with his penknife and his dog Dardo, was in the habit of going on outings in the morning. He would barely glance at me, and if he did so it was to demand something of me or scold me for something. His attitude, rather similar to that of Juan Alberto and Esperanza, did not offend me to the same extent. I admired him. After many subterfuges I managed to dress in a way that brought me luck. The clothing consisted of some short, baggy trousers of the kind the gauchos wear, a linen shirt, and some rubber boots I'd been given. One day during Carnival, taking advantage of the need to dress up, I put on that male clothing, which stood out more than Esperanza's disguise as a gardener. Horacio began treating me as if I were one of his male friends. To treat me like one of his friends was at times to mistreat me badly. He would often invite me to go horseback riding. When he needed to pee, he would do so right in front of me, without hiding at all, while we watched the lines of ants. We had conversations we would never have dared to have in front of other people. Two or three times we went swimming in the round metal tank without telling anyone. To seem more manly I stripped to the waist. At nap time, in the afternoon, I would escape to his room to tell him and his brothers about the conversations I had overheard in the kitchen and to describe to them what Elsa did at night by the mirror before going to bed. I never thought that that intimacy with

Horacio could prove so costly to me.

Juan Alberto said that dogs were like people: that when one of them was hurt, all of the others would jump on it to finish it off. Luis said that dogs were much better than people; that people were like monkeys, who imitate one another. Horacio said that each person resembles some animal, or that each animal ends up looking like a person, and that it was ridiculous to compare monkeys and dogs. Miss Domicia resembled a camel; Elsa a rabbit; Mr Ildefonso, in profile, a buffalo; Kaminsky the engineer, a donkey. Esperanza became indignant and, after some protests in favour of her parents, said that men all resembled owls, because they hissed at people at night to make them be quiet. I said the only thing I could think of: that men were like cicadas, but I couldn't say why. Then, when nobody heard me, in the middle of all the shouting, I said that they resembled cicadas because they were so noisy.

The boredom I felt when I was with Esperanza made the time seem longer. I often felt that I was about to faint, when Mlle Gabrielle would take us to her favourite place under the trees to give us our lessons. There, in the shade of a linden tree, she would open a knitting bag and take out balls of yarn, pieces of fabric, cookies and thread, a broken book. Everybody knew that Mlle Gabrielle was untidy: wherever she went she left behind bits of thread, fabric, wool, cookie crumbs. When she scolded us for leaving a loose end, she would blush, feeling she had no right to demand of others what she failed to do herself. She was good, blond, pale, and had a moustache. She taught me to read; she taught me some rudiments of French and mathematics; she also taught me some fables, which she forced me to recite for Mrs Celina's birthday.

Mlle Gabrielle made us take turns reading aloud from an illustrated book she herself had coloured in. The days I had to endure these readings were unlucky ones for me. Some disaster always happened, the direct product of my ill-humour or my disagreement. One such day I intentionally destroyed the diary of Juan Alberto, who thought of himself as an adult, someone worthy of respect because he had a diary. In the tiny pages I had read the ridiculous notes: *January 22nd I bought five packs of cigarettes and a tennis racket; January 23rd, had a shot of rum; January 24th, Luisita looked at me when I went past her door; January 25th, having a tooth pulled is horrible.*

When he found out I had destroyed his diary he did not say anything, but I guessed his intentions by looking in the depths of his eyes: he planned to wait for the right moment and then take his revenge in some nasty way. All day long I tried to be friendly to him, to agree with him about everything, but I knew that whatever I did to avoid his vengeance would only help bring it about.

Juan Alberto was eleven years old. I think boys are the cruelest at that age; girls start much earlier, at eight or nine, an age I had not yet attained.

We awaited the arrival of Mrs Celina. A telegram had announced her coming. I had not dared to say that she would return, something I had foreseen long before the telegram arrived. They began waxing the floors early in the morning. Mlle Gabrielle, Esperanza and I went to get flowers and peaches from the orchard. We put the peaches in a blue porcelain plate and the prettiest flowers in a crystal dish. We took advantage of the occasion to eat peaches, nuts, and two or three squares of chocolate, the kind that Mlle Gabrielle had ordered several bars of to make the desserts that were such a success.

Those exceptional days, when one could eat at times other than regular meal hours, you might have said I was crazy about any kind of food; you could say the food contained something that made me drunk, since when I ate I started laughing without being able to stop, with a high nervous laughter. The joy of seeing Mrs Celina again manifested itself in numerous acts of absent-mindedness, in the plates of food and in the flowers that Mlle Gabrielle picked.

To anyone who was willing to listen I described a doll I had imagined, with brown curls, blue eyes, a straw hat and a light-blue organdy dress. It said "Mommy" and "Daddy" over and over.

At nap time I took advantage of the state of confusion that filled the house to escape with Horacio. Without hats, we walked beneath the afternoon sun toward the round metal tank where we were planning to swim. Horacio took off his sandals, his trousers and his shirt; I had also stripped, but still had on my sandals and a handkerchief that I knotted around my head as a hair band. We climbed up on the corrugated metal to enjoy the dirty water before diving in; all of a sudden

Horacio said he saw a snake and that he would kill it. He jumped down on the ground, and I let myself fall down after him. The snake glided away and disappeared in the weeds. We searched for it on our knees. For some time Horacio had been looking for a coral snake to capture in a bottle: the one that afternoon was the first coral snake he'd found. He had seen them in illustrations in books. We peed, I squatting down on a slope and Horacio standing next to me; then, squatting in the grass, in the same posture, which Horacio said attracted reptiles, we were hoping to capture the snake when we heard a voice aimed at us: "Here they are." We turned around. Next to us was Juan Alberto; a little farther on, under a black umbrella, was Miss Domicia. Motionless, without realizing what was happening, we looked at each other. Juan Alberto pointed at us and said: "They're always up to the same thing." Miss Domicia, whose face was hidden by the fabric of the umbrella, gave a sort of grunt and turned around, telling Juan Alberto to follow her. The solitude and the heat embraced us once more. Horacio shrugged and resumed looking for the snake. I got dressed, watching the dark threatening clouds in the sky. Without speaking to Horacio, I went running to the house; I went to my room and threw myself on the bed. I was unable to think about the doll!

A big storm was gathering. I felt relieved when I heard the first thunder. "Perhaps the flood will come all at once and I'll be saved from my shame," I thought. I heard a lot of running around the courtyard, then the rain and the banging of shutters. I heard the bell at four o'clock, then the sound of tea cups and spoons, announcing it was time for tea. I didn't dare leave my room. After a time that seemed an eternity to me, Mlle Gabrielle came looking for me. I looked at her in terror. I soon saw that she wasn't unhappy with me; I got up from bed to follow her, after combing my hair and getting dressed as fast as I could. In the pantry Esperanza was sitting at the table. I sat down without speaking to her; to calm myself I imagined I had dreamt the whole scene that afternoon. There were just a few more hours until Mrs Celina would arrive. Mr Ildefonso, Juan Alberto, and Luis would go meet her in a carriage. I drank my tea submissively. After tea, when I was crossing the courtyard, I heard them talking about Horacio and then talking about me in connection with him. The story had passed from mouth to mouth and would reach Mrs Celina's ears and she would stop protecting me with her distant smile.

"We'll have to tell her," Miss Domicia was saying.

"Will you dare?" Doña Saturna responded.

"I couldn't rest if I didn't do it. I'd have it on my conscience."

"And who'll pick up the pieces?" Saturna asked.

"I don't know. I don't care," Domicia said. "This will teach her not to collect what isn't hers. They already have enough children without looking for more. I wash my hands of it all."

The sound of a carriage, in the midst of the rain, interrupted the dialogue. The horses stopped before the entrance to the courtyard of the house. Mr Ildefonso, wearing his glasses and holding an open umbrella, prepared to greet his wife. Esperanza ran to her mother's arms before anyone else. Juan Alberto and Luis came out, banging the doors behind them. Horacio came last of all. I stood behind a column, watching what I thought was the beginning of a tragedy. All of them took the traveller's cardboard boxes, packages, and suitcases out of the carriage, while she stepped on the foot-board of the carriage wearing a green rubber raincoat. Mrs Celina looked hard at the house, up and down as if she were seeing it for the first time. She kissed her children, pausing to take off a glove, to smooth her hair or shake her raincoat, covered with drops of water.

When she kissed Horacio she saw me behind the column and called me. I slowly approached her to receive her kiss. She handed me a cardboard box, asking me to open it and see what was inside. Surprised that I was not provoking the aversion I expected, I opened the box and found the doll with brown curls, blue eyes, a straw hat, and a light-blue organdy dress. I shook it. The doll said, "Daddy," "Mommy," in a soft moan. They advised me to take it out of the box by removing some strings that held it in place like a prisoner. Since I didn't dare to do it, Mrs Celina pulled it out of its prison herself.

"Witch," Mrs Celina told me.

"*Sorcière*," Mlle Gabrielle told me.

Both of them recognized the doll I had described.

That was how they pointed me toward the difficult art of soothsaying.

The Punishment

We were facing a mirror that reflected our faces and the flowers in the room.

"What's the matter?" I asked her. She was pale. "Are you concealing something from me?"

"I don't conceal anything from you. That mirror reminds me of my misfortune: that we are two and not one person," she said, covering her face. "When I see you looking so severe, I feel guilty. Everything seems like infidelity to me. I'm twenty years old. What good is that? For fear of losing me, you don't want me to look at anything, to try anything; you don't want me to live. You want me to be yours once and for all, like an inanimate object. If I went along with you, I'd end up retreating to the first moments of my life or be driven to the point of death, or perhaps I'd go crazy," she told me. "Aren't you scared of that?"

"You're concealing something from me," I insisted. "Don't try distracting my attention with your complaints."

"If you really think I'm concealing something from you, I'll go through everything that has happened to me in the last twenty years, my whole life. I'll sum it all up."

"As if I didn't know the story of your life!" I answered.

"You don't know it. Let me rest my head on your knees, because I feel sleepy."

I settled into the sofa and let her rest comfortably on me, rocking her as if she were a newborn.

"The only sin that existed for me was infidelity. But—how to be faithful without being dead to the rest of the world and to yourself? In a room with flowers painted on the wall, Sergio held me naked in his arms. He suspected I had deceived him and he wanted to kill me. I hadn't deceived him, for in my unfaithfulness, if such a thing existed, I'd been searching for him."

"Why do you name me as if you were speaking of someone else?"

"Because Sergio was someone else. For three years I knew perfect love. Everything united us: we had the same tastes, the same character, the same sensibility. He controlled me: he devoured me the way a tiger devours a lamb. He loved me as if he had me inside him, and I loved him as if I had come from him. At the end of three years of joy and also of torture, we learned, little by little, in ways ever more romantic and modest, how not to know even how to kiss each other. Shame covered my body, like a dress that's too tight, with too many snaps and ties. I refused to see him any more. I felt repelled by his kisses. He wrote me a letter suggesting obscene things to me. I threw the letter in the fire. 'What will be inside this letter?' I thought when I saw the envelope, full of hope. I held it in my hands for a while before opening it.

"We arranged to meet in a church; we hardly looked at each other. Later, furtively, in a square. For a time I lived enveloped in a sort of fog, disturbing yet fortunate.

"Some months later I met Sergio in a theatre."

"Don't name me as if you didn't know me. I feel as though I could strangle you," I told her. She continued as if she hadn't heard me:

"How handsome a stranger is! I was moved to see those eyes looking at me for the first time. I trembled with emotion, like someone who sees the beginning of spring in a single tiny leaf at a time when the rest of the garden is still sunken in winter, or like someone who sees a cliff amidst blue mountains and bushes with dazzling, distant flowers. Vertigo, I felt only vertigo. Surely we'd met in some previous incarnation: we didn't greet each other, and yet it seemed natural to me. 'I would like to know him in this life,' I thought with some vehemence. Swiftly I forgot Sergio."

"I forbid you to play with our love," I told her, trying to catch her attention; she didn't listen to me.

"I was happy, with that happiness produced by anticipation. I danced before the mirror. I played the piano incredibly well, at least that's what I thought. I was waiting for—what? I don't know. For a boyfriend, no doubt. I was already tired of studying. Not even bashfulness saved me from tedium, from nervousness during exams. My philosophy teacher was my best friend. I brought her bouquets of roses, or flowers that I brought from the countryside. She invited me to tea at her house. She stopped being my friend. She treated me with scorn or indifference.

"'Take a bouquet of flowers to your teacher; if you don't pay attention to her, she'll never show you any kindness,' my mother told me one day.

"'Does kindness have to be bought?'

"'Who taught you that ugly word?' she said to me.

"'Which one?' I asked, in obvious bad faith.

"'Bought. You buy fruit, food, clothing, God knows what, but not human feelings,' she answered proudly.

"'Everything can be bought, with or without money,' I told her.

"I don't know why I remember that conversation so exactly. The days were getting longer, wider, deeper. There was time for everything, mostly for forgetting. It took me a long time to forget how to dance or play the piano. My body lost its balance; when I tried to stand on tiptoe I wobbled; my fingers lost their agility, got stuck on the notes when they ran over the scales. I felt humiliated. I tried to kill myself one winter night, sitting naked by an open window, motionless, shivering with cold, until dawn; later, with a sleeping pill I bought under the counter at a drugstore; later, with a revolver I found in my father's room. Everything failed because of my indecisiveness, my nervousness, my good health, but not because of any love for life. Alicia disappointed me with her betrayals, with her lies. I resolved not to see her any more and, before parting from her, to tell her sins to the whole of her family, one day when they were all together, in front of those mystical paintings so carefully illuminated in their living room. Alicia and I confided in one another. She was my best friend. We slept together in the summertime with mosquito nets covering our faces.

We always fell in love with the same boy, who was always in love with me. Alicia thought they were in love with her. We got annoyed with each other for no reason. We laughed at everything and for any cause whatsoever: at death, at love, at misfortune and at happiness. We didn't know what we wanted, and what we most enjoyed sometimes turned out to be tedious and boring.

"'These kids think they're grown-ups,' my mother would say, or my aunt, or one of the servants; 'they need a good beating.'

"We read pornographic books that we hid under the mattress, we smoked, we went to the movies instead of studying.

"We swam every morning at the municipal pool, and won prizes in four or five races. We also swam in the river, when we were invited to spend the day in some resort at Tigre; or in the sea, that summer we spent in a house my aunt rented at Los Acantilados. I saw the sea for the first time! There we learned to float on the water, learning with some difficulty because we were afraid. We were forgetting how to swim. Oh, how we sank in the water! One day we almost drowned, hanging onto each other, trying to save ourselves or pull each other under.

"'You're going to drown,' my mother warned me. 'When you learn to swim, you'll lose your fear, and will be able to win swimming races.' In my chest of drawers I collected postcards I received from Claudina. I couldn't sleep just from thinking about going to school: shame before the other children, fear of the older ones, curiosity about sexual pangs, everything tormented me.

"We spent days and days of happiness in a huge garden with two stone sphinxes that guarded the entrance by the gate. In the afternoon we went down to the river for a walk. From the road to the Yacht Club you could see the church of San Isidro, where they took me to hear Mass on Sundays. I was a mystic, devoted to the Virgin of Lujan. Instead of wearing a bracelet on my wrist, I wore a rosary. Claudina went to Europe. We bought fresh eggs in a little house hidden behind a gigantic vine. Sometimes they let me go on a bicycle, with Claudina or by myself. During one of my outings a man looked at my tiny breasts and said obscene things to me. I was frightened and told Claudina about it. I wasn't used to having breasts. Time passed and the bicycle became extremely tall for me. I lacked the balance necessary to ride it.

"'Fraidy cat,' the gardener would say to me, looking at my knees and stroking his moustache.

"The scar I have on my forehead is from a blow I gave myself on a post when I was going down the hill.

"I took my first Communion. I dreamed about my white dress. I had a straight body—no hips, no breasts, no waist—like a boy's. They took us, Claudina and me, to the photographer's house, dressed in white tulle, bearing missals and evil thoughts. I still have the pictures.

"I remember the day the new bicycle arrived at our house, still in its crate. And later, the day my mother promised it to me if I got good grades in school. 'Riding on a tricycle is boring! When do I get a bicycle?' my voice said.

"I went round and round the furniture in the house on my tricycle, thinking about that bicycle. We were in town.

"With a crewcut, like a boy, I climbed trees. I was convalescing only slowly, for my mother could not get me to keep still. Three doctors surrounded my bed. I heard them talking about typhus. I was shaking in bed and constantly drinking water and orange juice. My mother was frightened: her eyes shone like precious stones. A doctor must be called.

"That same morning she said: 'My daughter doesn't have anything. She has an iron constitution,' and she sent me to school with the nursemaid.

"I was drinking water from a swamp full of garbage the day I met Claudina. Nobody ever spoke of my prank.

"I didn't yet know how to ride a tricycle. The pedals hurt my legs.

"We took a trip to France: the sea, which I saw for the last time, fascinated me. And later, for a long time, I asked my mother: 'What will France be like? What's the sea like?'

"I pretended to read the newspaper, like the adults did, sitting in a chair. Rosa, Magdalena, and Ercilia were my friends. We were all the same age, but I was the most precocious. I could recognize any tune. In the swings at Palermo Park, I swung without any fear, and would climb the tallest slide without a moment's hesitation. Then, little by little, they no longer allowed me to climb any but the lowest slide, because the other one was dangerous. Danger, danger: what was danger? They tried to teach me what it was: with knives, with pins, with broken glass, with electric outlets, with heights. They did not allow me to eat chocolate or ice cream or go on the merry-go-round by myself.

"'Why can't I eat chocolate?' I would ask. 'Because it will give you in-digestion,' they would answer. I adored my mother: I cried when she didn't come back from the street early. My friends stole my toys.

"Someone scared me one night with a stuffed monkey, and the next day gave me the same monkey, which I didn't like. People made me afraid or happy. I didn't know how to write except with rubber blocks: rose, house, mommy. The days got longer and longer. Each day includ-ed little dawns, little afternoons, little evenings, repeated over and over. I cried when I saw a dog or a cat that wasn't a toy. I couldn't recognize the letters: not even the O or the A, that were so easy; I couldn't recognize the numbers, not even zero that looked like an egg, or one that looked like a little soldier. I started tasting certain fruits and soups for the first time; then the sweet taste of milk. This is my life," she told me, closing her eyes. "Remembering the past is killing me."

"Are you making fun of me?" I asked her.

She didn't answer. Her lips closed: she never opened them again to say she loved me. I couldn't cry. As if I were watching her from the top of a mountain, I watched her, distant, defenceless, unassailable. Her madness was my only rival. I embraced her for the last time and it was like a rape. During her story, time had run backwards for me: twenty years less for her had meant twenty more for me. I took a look in the mirror, hoping that it would reflect less afflicted, less demented be-ings than ourselves. I saw that my hair had turned white.

The Basement

This basement, exceedingly cold in winter, is an Eden in the summertime. Some people sit by the door upstairs searching for some cool air on the hottest days in January, dirtying the floor. No window lets in the light or the horrible heat of the day. I have a large mirror, a couch or cot given me by a client who was a millionaire, and four mattresses I have acquired over the years from other girls. In the morning I fill pails (lent me by the doorman of the next building) with water to wash my face and hands. I'm very clean. I have a hanger for my clothes behind a drape, and a mantel for the candlesticks. There is no electricity or water. My night table is a chair, and my chair is a velvet pillow. One of my clients, the youngest one, brought bits of old curtains from his grandmother's house, and I use them to decorate the walls, along with pictures I cut from the magazines. The lady upstairs feeds me lunch; for breakfast I have candy or whatever I can stuff in my pockets. I have to live with mice, and at first it seemed to me that was the only defect of this basement, where I don't have to pay rent. Now I have noticed that these animals are not so terrible; they are quite discreet. When all's said and done they're preferable to flies, so abundant in the fanciest houses in Buenos Aires, those places where they used to give me leftovers when I was eleven. While the clients are here the mice keep out of sight: they know the difference between one kind of silence and another. As soon as I am alone they come out in an uproar. They go running by, stopping for a moment and looking at me out of a corner of their eyes, as if they guessed what I think of them. Sometimes they eat a bit of cheese or bread from the floor. They're not afraid of me, nor I of them. The worst of it is that I can't store any provisions because they eat them before I have a chance to try anything myself. There are evil-minded people who are pleased at this turn of events and call me Fermina, the Mouse Lady. I don't feel like humouring them and so refuse to ask them to lend me traps to kill the mice. One of them, the oldest one, is named Charlie Chaplin, another is Gregory Peck, another Marlon Brando, another Duilio Marzio; one that is very playful is named Daniel Gellin, another is Yul Brynner, one female is Gina Lollobrigida and another is Sophia Loren. It is strange how these little animals have taken possession of a basement where no doubt they lived before I arrived. Even the damp spots on the wall have taken the form of mice; they are dark and rather long, with two little ears and a long pointed tail. When nobody is watching, I gather food for them in one of the saucers given me by the man who lives in the house across the way. I don't want them to leave me. If some neighbour comes and wants to exterminate them with traps or a cat, I'll make a scandal he'll never forget as long as he lives. They have announced that this house will be torn down, but I won't leave here until I die. Up above they're packing trunks and baskets and incessantly making packages. There are moving vans by the front door, but I walk by them as if I didn't see them. I never begged for a cent from those gentlemen. They spy on me all day long and believe I am with clients because I talk to myself to annoy them. Since they're angry with me, they lock me in; since I'm angry with them, I don't ask them to open the door. For the last two days the mice have been acting very strangely: one brought me a ring, another a bracelet, and a third, the sharpest one, brought me a necklace. At first I couldn't believe it, and nobody else will believe it. I'm happy. What does it matter if it's all a dream? I'm thirsty: I drink my own sweat. I'm hungry: I chew on my fingers and my hair. The police won't come looking for me. They won't ask me for a health certificate or a certificate of good conduct. The ceiling is falling in, bits of straw are floating down: it must be the beginning of the demolition. I hear cries and none of them are my name. The mice are afraid. Poor things! They don't know, don't understand the way the world is. They don't know the joy of revenge. I look at myself in a little mirror: in all the time I have looked at myself in the mirror I have never been so beautiful.

The Guests

For winter vacation, Lucio's parents had planned a trip to Brazil. They wanted to show Lucio the Corcovado, the Sugarloaf, and Tijuca, and to admire the sights afresh through their child's eyes.

Lucio fell ill with German measles: that's not too serious, but "with his face and arms looking like grits," as his mother said, he couldn't travel.

They decided to leave him in the care of an old servant, a very fine woman. Before their departure they recommended that she buy a cake with candles for the child's birthday, which was coming up, even if his little friends wouldn't be able to come and share in it: they wouldn't be coming to the party because of the inevitable fear of contagion.

Joyfully, Lucio said goodbye to his parents: he thought that farewell would bring him nearer his birthday, which was so important for him. To comfort him, even though there was no need to comfort him, his parents promised to bring him a painting of the Corcovado made of butterfly wings, a wooden knife with a view of the Sugarloaf painted on the handle, and a telescope through which one could see the most important sights of Rio de Janeiro, with its palm trees, or of Brasilia, with its red earth.

The day consecrated to happiness, in Lucio's hopes, was slow in coming. Vast zones of sadness impeded its arrival, but one morning, so different for him from other mornings, the cake with six candles (which the servant had bought, obeying the instructions of the lady of the house) finally sparkled on the table in Lucio's room. Also, by the front door, a new bicycle gleamed, painted yellow, a present left by his parents.

There's nothing so infuriating as unnecessary waiting: that was why the servant tried to celebrate the birthday, light the candles, and enjoy the cake at lunch time, but Lucio protested, saying that his guests would come in the afternoon.

"In the afternoon, cake seems heavier on the digestion, just as an orange in the morning is of gold, in the afternoon of silver and at night is deadly. The guests won't come," the servant added. "Their mothers won't let them come, for fear of contagion. They already told your mother."

Lucio refused to listen to reason. After the squabble, the servant and the child did not speak until tea time.

She took a nap and he looked out the window, waiting.

At five o'clock there was a knocking at the door. The servant went to open it, thinking it was a delivery boy or a messenger. But Lucio knew who was knocking. It could not be anyone but his guests. He smoothed his hair while looking at himself in the mirror, then changed his shoes and washed his hands. A group of impatient girls was waiting with their mothers.

"No boys amongst the guests. How strange!" the servant exclaimed. "What's your name?" she asked one of the girls, who looked nicer than the others.

"My name is Livia."

The others said their names all at once and came in.

"Ladies, please come in and sit down," the servant told the women, who obeyed right away.

Lucio paused by the door to his room. He already looked more grown up! One by one, looking them in the eye, looking at their hands and feet, taking a step backward to be able to see them better, he greeted the girls.

Alicia was wearing a tight-fitting wool dress, and a knit cap, the old kind that's back in fashion. She looked like an old woman and smelled of camphor. When she took out her handkerchief, mothballs fell out of her pockets, but she gathered them up and put them back in. She was no doubt precocious, since the expression on her face showed a profound preoccupation with everything that was happening around her. She was worried about the other girls pulling on her hair ribbons, and about a package she grasped tightly under her arm and refused to put down anywhere. This package contained the birthday present. A present that poor Lucio would never receive.

Livia was exuberant. Her glance seemed to catch on fire and then go out like that of those dolls that run on batteries. As exuberant as she was affectionate, she hugged Lucio and took him into a corner, to tell him a secret: the present she was bringing him. She did not need any words to speak: that detail, unpleasant for everyone but Lucio, seemed a jest played on the others. In a tiny box, which she unwrapped herself, since she couldn't stand the slowness with which Lucio unwrapped it, there were two crude magnetized dolls, who could not resist kissing, mouth to mouth, their necks straining, whenever they got within a certain distance of each other. For a long while the little girl showed Lucio how to play with the dolls in such a way that their postures would be more perfect or more strange. Inside the same little box there was a partridge that whistled and a green crocodile. The presents—or the girl's charms—totally captivated Lucio's attention. He neglected the rest of the delegation, and hid in a corner of the house with the dolls and Livia.

Irma, her hands forming fists, her lips pursed, her skirt torn, and her knees scraped, infuriated by Lucio's reception, by his preference for the presents of the exuberant girl who was whispering in the corner, hit Lucio in the face with the force of a boy, and, not satisfied with this, kicked the partridge and the crocodile, which had been left on the floor, to pieces, while the girls' mothers, a bunch of hypocrites, according to the servant, lamented the disaster that had occurred on such an important day.

The servant lit the candles on the cake and closed the curtains so that the mysterious light of the flames would shine more brightly. A brief silence brought life to the ritual. But Lucio did not cut the cake or blow out the candles as custom required him to do. A scandal occurred: Milona stuck in the knife and Elvira blew out the candles.

Angela, who was dressed in a suit of organdy adorned with lace

inserts and hems, was distant and cold: she refused to try even a tiny
piece of the icing for the cake, or even look at it; at her house, according to her, the birthday cakes contained surprises. She refused to
drink a cup of hot chocolate because it had some scum on it, and
when they brought her the strainer she got offended and, saying she
was no baby, threw it all on the floor. She didn't notice, or pretended
not to notice, the struggle between Lucio and the two girls who had
crushes on him (she was stronger than Irma, or so she said), nor did
she take note of the fuss provoked by Milona and Elvira, because, as
she said, only idiots go to silly parties, and she preferred to think
about other, happier, birthdays.

"Why do these girls come to parties if they don't want to talk to
anybody, if they sit by themselves, if they look down on the dishes that
have been prepared with such love? Even as little girls they're party
poopers," the offended servant complained to Alicia's mother.

"Don't get upset," the lady answered, "they're all the same."

"Why shouldn't I get upset! They have a lot of nerve: they blow out
the candles and cut the cake without even being the birthday child."

Milona was very pink.

"I don't have any trouble making her eat," her mother said, licking
her lips. "Don't even try giving her dolls or books because she won't
look at them. She asks for candies and pastries. Even ordinary quince
jam drives her mad with pleasure. Her favourite game is having
snacks."

Elvira was very ugly. Oily black hair covered her eyes. She never
looked straight at anything. A green colour like that of olives covered
her cheeks; no doubt she had a bad liver. When she saw the only present that was still on the table, she let out a shrill laugh.

"Girls who give ugly things for presents should be punished. Isn't
that right, Mommy?" she said to her mother.

When she went by the table, with her long tangled hair she managed to sweep the two dolls off onto the floor, where they kept on
kissing one another.

"Teresa, Teresa," the guests called out.

Teresa did not answer. She was as indifferent as Angela, but did not
sit up as straight, and barely opened her eyes. Her mother said she was
sleepy: she had sleeping sickness. She pretends to be asleep.

"She even sleeps when she's having fun. It's nice because she leaves me in peace," she added.

Teresa was not completely ugly; at times she even seemed friendly, but she was monstrous if one compared her with the other girls. She had heavy eyelids and a double chin not in keeping with her age. At times she seemed very good, but then one was disabused of that idea: when one of the girls fell on the floor, she didn't come to her aid, but stayed stretched out in her chair, groaning, looking at the ceiling, saying she was tired.

"What a birthday party," the servant thought after it was over. "Only one guest brought a present. Let's not mention the rest of it. One ate almost the whole cake; another broke the toys and hurt Lucio; another went off with the present she brought; another said unpleasant things, of the kind that only adults say, and with a dough-like face didn't say goodbye to me when she left; another stayed sitting in a corner like a poultice, without any blood in her veins; and another (God help me! I think it was the one named Elvira), had a viper-like face that looks like it must bring bad luck; but I think Lucio fell in love with one of them, the one with the present, just out of self-interest. She knew how to win him over even without being pretty. Women are worse than men. It's hopeless."

When Lucio's parents came back from their trip, they never found out who the girls were who had visited him on his birthday, and they thought their son had secret relations, which was, and probably still is, true.

But by then Lucio was a little man.

Carl Herst

Carl Herst had a very broad face, prominent cheek- and jawbones, sunken eyes. My brother wanted to buy a dog from him. He lived in Olivos and we went to see the dog. When we arrived at the house, Carl Herst himself opened the door. He made us go straight to his study. There we sat down and drank cold beer; he spoke to us at length about his breeding program, of how much work it was, of the animals' pedigree, and of the importance of proper feeding.

He went to the back of the yard in search of Fulo (that was the name of the dog he had available to sell to my brother) and we stayed behind looking around the room. On the walls, there were photographs in golden frames, all of them of dogs; on the tables, the picture frames had photographs of hairless dogs, hairy dogs, dogs in groups, by themselves, midgets, very tall ones, long ones like sausages, pug-nosed ones with moonlike faces, mothers and children, siblings, all ages. In a half-open album I glimpsed collections of snapshots, also of dogs: in the countryside, in the city, running, sitting, lying down. When Carl Herst arrived with Fulo, my brother and I were laughing, but I soon stopped laughing because the animal scared me. He had a huge jaw and cold, round eyes.

"Is he fierce?" I asked.

"He's very good," Herst answered, "and very loyal."

After discussing the price, my brother decided we would come back the next day.

The next day there wasn't anybody home when we arrived, but a neighbour told us the gentleman had said we should go to the back of the yard if we wanted to take the dog. We went to the end of the yard where there was a cyclone fence and, inside the fence, a large and well-appointed wooden doghouse. Trembling, I followed my brother. We went in through a little iron door with peeling paint. The dogs looked at us in a friendly way, and Fulo came running over. Then he went into the doghouse. My brother went into the doghouse to find him; I peered in from outside. On the inside walls, painted white, I saw a picture hanging. I looked at it intently: it was a photograph of Carl Herst.

On the walls there were plates hanging with inscriptions such as: "What dog is like a friend?" "Love men; take care of them; they are part of your soul." "I have a friend; what else matters?" "When you feel alone don't seek another dog." "Man does not betray you, dogs will." "A man never lies."

Magush

A Thessalian witch read the future of Polycrates in the designs the
surf made on its way down the beach; a Roman vestal virgin read that
of Caesar in a little pile of sand by a plant; Cornelius Agrippa of
Germany used a mirror to read the future. Some present-day
sorcerers read one's destiny in tea leaves or in the dregs of coffee at the
bottom of a cup; some read it in trees, in rain, in ink-blots or egg
whites, others simply in the lines of the palm, others in crystal balls.
Magush reads the future in a vacant building opposite the charcoal
yard where he lives. The six huge picture windows and the twelve little windows of the adjacent building are like cards for him. Magush
never thought of associating windows and cards: that was my idea. His
methods are mysterious and can be explained only in part. He tells
me that during the day he has trouble drawing conclusions, because
the light disturbs the images. The most propitious moment to carry
out his task is at sunset, when certain slanting rays of light filter
through the inside windows of the building and are reflected on the
glass of the windows in front. That is why he always makes appoint-
ments with his clients for the same hour. I know, I have found out after
long research, that the upper part of the building has to do with matters of the heart, the lower part with money and work, and the middle

with problems of family and health.

Magush, despite the fact that he's only fourteen, is a friend of mine. I met him by chance one day when I went to buy a sack of charcoal. I wasn't slow to guess his gift of prophecy. After several conversations in the patio of the charcoal yard (surrounded by sacks of charcoal, freezing to death), he asked me into the room where he works. The room is a sort of hallway, just as chilly as the patio; from there, through a combination of skylights of coloured glass and of a tall narrow window (just the shape for a giraffe), the facing building can easily be seen, its yellowing façade marked by rain and sun. After a while in the room I found the chill was departing and a pleasant feeling of warmth was replacing it. Magush told me that this phenomenon occurs during the moments of prophecy, and that it is not the room but the body that absorbs those beneficent rays.

Magush was extraordinarily courteous to me. At the propitious moment, he let me look at the windows of the building myself, one by one. (Incomprehensible scenes were sometimes visible; in that respect, I was lucky at first.) In one of the windows I saw, for my sins, she who later became my fiancee, with my rival. She was wearing the red dress I found dazzling, her hair loose except for a little bun on the back of her neck. To see that detail I might have needed the eyes of a lynx, but the sharpness of the image was due to the magic that surrounded it and not to my eyesight. (At the same distance I've been able to read letters or newspaper clippings.) There I saw the painful scene I later had to suffer in the flesh. There I saw that bed covered with pink blankets and the horrible ladies going in and out with packages. There, in the window aglow at sunset, I saw the excursions to Tigre and to the Lujan River. There I was about to strangle someone. Later, when I met up with these events, the reality seemed a little faded to me, and my fiancee perhaps less beautiful.

After those experiences, my interest in living what was destined for me diminished. I consulted with Magush. Was it possible to avoid? To refrain from living—was that possible? Magush, who is intelligent, thought about whether it was worthwhile trying to do that. For several days I didn't leave his side. I entertained myself watching images, refraining from searching them out and living them. Magush said that because of our friendship of many years he was making an exception; he would never have allowed anyone else to do that. I entertained myself watching my destiny appear in those windows and Magush playing tricks on his clients, whom he gave my destiny as if it were their own.

"It's more prudent to have someone live out your destiny right away, as soon as it appears in the windows. Otherwise it might come looking for you: destiny is like a man-eating tiger lying in ambush for its owner," Magush would say to me. He would add, in order to reassure me: "One day, perhaps, there'll be no more of you in those windows."

"Will I die?" I asked uneasily.

"Not necessarily," answered Magush. "You can live without a destiny."

"But even dogs have a destiny," I protested.

"Dogs can't avoid it: they're obedient."

What Magush had foretold happened in part, and I lived for a time bored and calm, devoted to my work. But life attracted me, and I missed it while standing by Magush, watching the building. The figures intended to elucidate my destiny had still not gone out. In each window we were sometimes surprised by new, inextricable designs. Sombre lights, ghosts with the faces of dogs, criminals: everything indicated that it would be better if those pictures I saw did not come true.

"Who would want to live out those misfortunes?" I asked Magush. He resolved one day, in order to distract me, to become at once an adviser and a magician. I began to see fireworks, puppets, Japanese lanterns, dwarfs, people dressed as bears and as cats. I said to him hypocritically: "I envy you. I wish I were fourteen."

"I'll switch destinies with you," Magush said.

I accepted, although his proposal seemed impertinent to me. What would I do with those dwarfs? We talked too long about the difficulties that might be entailed in the difference in our ages. Perhaps we lost the faith we needed.

Our project was not carried out. Both of us missed the chance to satisfy our curiosity.

Sometimes we feel the renewed temptation to switch destinies; we give it a try, but always come up against the same obstacle: if I think about the difficulties Magush has overcome, the idea seems absurd. Not long ago I was about to leave. I packed my bags. We said goodbye. The images in the windows were tempting. Something stopped me at the last moment. The same thing happened to Magush: he didn't have the nerve to escape from the charcoal yard.

I'm always fascinated by Magush's destiny and he by mine (no matter how bad it is), but at bottom the only thing that both of us want is to keep contemplating the windows of the building and giving others our destinies, as long as they don't seem extraordinary to us.

The Prayer

Laura was in church, praying:

Oh my God, won't you reward the good deeds of Your servant? I know that at times I wasn't good. I'm impatient and deceitful. I lack charity, but I always try to merit Your forgiveness. Haven't I spent hours kneeling on the floor of my room before the image of one of Your Virgins? This horrible child I've hidden in my house, to save him from those who wanted to lynch him, won't he bring me any satisfaction? I have no children, I'm an orphan, I'm not in love with my husband, all this You know well. I don't hide anything from You. My parents led me to marriage as one leads a girl to school or to the doctor. I obeyed them because I thought everything would turn out all right. I don't hide it from You: love can't be forced, and even if You Yourself had given me the command to love my husband, I wouldn't be able to obey You unless You inspired the love in me that I need. When he embraces me I want to run away, to hide in a forest (since childhood I have always imagined an enormous forest covered with snow where I hide when I am in distress). He tells me, "You're so cold. . . it's as if you were made of marble."

I much prefer the ugly box-office attendant who sometimes gives me tickets so I can go to the movies with my little sister, or the rather repulsive salesman in the shoe store who caresses my foot between his legs when I'm trying shoes on, or the blond bricklayer at the corner of Corrientes and July 9th Streets, next to the house where my favourite student lives, the one I like, the one with dark eyes who sits on the ground eating a steak sandwich, onions and grapes, the one who asks me: "Are you married?" and then says, without waiting for an answer, "What a shame."

The one who made me go in through the scaffolding to see the apartment that's to be occupied by a couple of newlyweds.

I visited the apartment under construction four times. The first time was in the morning; they were laying bricks for a partition. I sat on the pile of lumber. It was the house of my dreams. The bricklayer (whose name is Anselmo) took me to the highest part of the house so I could see the view. You know that Your servant had no desire to stay so long in the construction site and that it was only because she twisted her ankle that, without wanting to, she had to stay with the men for a long time, waiting for the pain to subside. The second time I arrived in the afternoon. They were installing the windows and I went looking for a change purse I had forgotten. Anselmo wanted me to see the terrace. It was six o'clock in the afternoon when we came down and all the other workers had left. While passing a wall I got whitewash on my arm and cheek. Anselmo, with his handkerchief, without asking my permission, rubbed off the spots. I saw that his eyes were blue and his mouth bright red. I looked at him, perhaps too hard, because he told me: "What eyes you have!"

We went down through the scaffolding holding hands. He asked me to return at eight o'clock the next night because one of his fellow workers was going to play the accordion and the wife of another was going to bring some wine. You know, oh my God, that I went not for my own sake but so as not to offend him. Anselmo's co-worker was playing the accordion when I arrived. By the light of a lantern the others were gathered around some bottles. The woman had brought a basket full of bottles of wine so we could drink, and we drank. I left before the party was over. Anselmo guided me with a lantern to the entrance. He wanted to accompany me for a few blocks. I didn't let him.

"Will you come back?" he said in parting. "You still haven't seen the tile work."

"What tile work?" I asked, laughing.

"In the bathroom," he answered, as if kissing me. "Come back, tomorrow they're coming."

"Who?"

"The newlyweds. We can spy on them."

"I'm not used to spying."

"I'll show you a neon sign, some shoes with wings. Did you ever see them?"

"No."

"I'll show you them tomorrow."

"O.K."

"Will you come?"

"Yes," I answered, and then I left.

The third time there wasn't anyone in the building. Behind a wooden fence there was a fire burning; a pot rested on some stones.

"Tonight I'm replacing the night watchman," he told me when he saw me coming.

"And the couple?"

"The couple has already left. Shall we go up to see the neon sign?"

"O.K.," I said, trying to hide my nervousness.

Oh my God, I had no idea what awaited me on the seventh floor. We went up. I thought my heart was beating because of having to climb so many stairs and not because I was alone in that building with that man. When we got to the top, I was happy to see the neon sign from the terrace. I was afraid. There was no railing and I retreated to the bedroom. Anselmo took me by the waist.

"Don't fall," he said, adding: "Here they're going to put the bed. It must be beautiful being married, having a place."

As he said these words he sat down on the floor next to a little suit-case and a bundle of clothing.

"Do you want to see some pictures? Sit down."

He put a newspaper on the floor so I could sit down. I sat down. He opened the suitcase and from inside it, oh my God, he took out an envelope, from which he took some pictures.

"This was my mother," he said, coming up close to me. "You can see how beautiful she was," addressing me now with the familiar form. "And this is my sister," he said, blowing lightly on my face.

He had me cornered and began embracing me without letting me

even breathe. Oh my God, You know I tried in vain to free myself from
his arms. You know I pretended to be hurt so as to force him to come
to his senses. You know I went away crying. I hide nothing from You.
I know I'm not virtuous, but do You know many virtuous women? I'm
not one of those who wear tight pants and have half their breasts
showing when they go to the riverside on Sunday. Of course my husband would be opposed to such things, but there are times I could
take advantage of his absent-mindedness and do them. I'm not to
blame if men look at me: they look at me as if I were a girl. I'm young,
that's true, but what they like about me is not that. They don't even
look at Rosaura or Clara when they walk down the street: they don't
get even one word of flattery during summer vacation, I'm sure of
that. Not even indecent remarks, the kind that are so easy to get. I'm
pretty: is that really a sin? It's worse to be embittered. Since marrying
Alberto, I've lived in that dark street in Avellaneda. You know very well
that it's not paved and that at night I twist my ankles on the way home
when I wear very high heels. On rainy days I wear rubber boots, all
worn out by now, and a raincoat that looks like a sack, to go to my job.
Of course sacks are in fashion now. I'm a piano teacher and could
have been a great pianist if it weren't for my husband, who is against
it, and because of my lack of vanity. Sometimes, when we have people
over, he insists I play tangos or jazz. Mortified, I sit down at the piano
and obey unwillingly, because I know he likes it. My life is without joy.
Every day, at the same hour, except on Saturdays and holidays, I go
down España Street to the house of one of my students. On a solitary
stretch of unpaved road, full of deep ruts, about three weeks ago (a
period that has seemed endless to me), I saw five boys playing. Absent-
mindedly I saw them in the mud, by a ditch, as though they were not
real children. Two of them were fighting: one had taken the other's
blue-and-yellow kite and was grasping it firmly to his chest. The other
took him by the neck (forcing him to fall into the ditch) and pushed
his head under water. They struggled for a few moments: one trying to
make the other's head stay under water, the other trying to pull it out.
Some bubbles appeared in the muddy water, as when we stick an empty bottle in water and it goes glug glug glug. Without releasing the
head, the boy kept holding onto his victim, who no longer had the
strength to defend himself. The playmates clapped their hands.
Sometimes minutes seem very long or very short. I watched the scene,

as if in the movie theatre, without thinking that I could intervene. When the boy released the head of his adversary, it sank into the silent mud. Then they scattered. The boys ran away. I discovered I had watched a crime, a crime in the midst of games that looked so innocent. Running, the boys reached their houses, where they announced that Amancio Araoz had been murdered by Claudio Herrera. I pulled Amancio out of the ditch. It was then that the women and men in the neighbourhood, armed with clubs and tools, wanted to lynch Claudio Herrera. Claudio's mother, who was very fond of me, asked me, sobbing, to hide him in my house, which I did willingly enough, after leaving the little corpse in the bed where they wrapped him in his shroud. My house was some distance from that of Amancio Araoz's parents and that made things easier. During the funeral people didn't cry over Amancio but instead cursed Claudio. Walking along, they went around the block with the coffin. They stopped by each doorway to yell insults against Claudio Herrera, so that people would know of the crime he had committed. They were so excited they looked happy. On Amancio's white coffin they had put bright flowers which the women constantly praised. Various children who were not related to the dead boy followed the procession to amuse themselves; they made a commotion, laughing, dragging sticks along the cobblestones. I don't think anybody cried; indignation requires no tears. Only one old lady, Miss Carmen, was sobbing, because she didn't understand what had happened. Oh my God, what stinginess, what a lack of ceremony there was in that funeral! Claudio Herrera is eight years old. It's impossible to know to what extent he is conscious of the crime he has committed. I protect him like a mother. I can't explain exactly why I feel so happy. I turned my living room into a bedroom for him. In the back of the house, where the chicken coop used to be, I made him a swing and a hammock; I bought him a bucket and a shovel so he can make a little garden and amuse himself with the plants. Claudio loves me or at least behaves as if he loves me. He obeys me more than he does his mother. I prohibited his going out on the balconies or the flat roof of the house. I banned his answering the telephone. He never disobeyed me. He helps me wash the dishes when we're done eating. He washes and peels the vegetables and sweeps the courtyard in the morning. I don't have any reason to complain; nevertheless, perhaps under the influence of the neighbours' opinion, I've begun to view

him as a criminal. I'm sure, oh my God, that in various different ways
he has tried to kill my dog Jasmine. First I noticed that he had put
cockroach poison in the plate where we put Jasmine's dinner; later, he
tried to drown her under the faucet or in the pail we use to wash the
courtyard. For the last few days I am convinced he did not give her any
water, or that if he did, it was mixed with ink, because Jasmine rejected
it immediately with much barking. I attribute her diarrhea to some
diabolical mixture he put in the meat we feed her. I consulted the doctor who always gives me advice. She knows that I have many medicines
in my medicine cabinet, among them barbiturates. The last time I
went to see her she told me: "Sweetheart, lock your medicine cabinet.
Children's crimes are dangerous. Children use any means to reach
their ends. They study dictionaries. Nothing gets by them. They know
everything. He could poison your husband, whom he loathes, according to what you've told me."

I replied: "For people to recover their goodness, it's necessary to
have faith in them. If Claudio suspects that I don't trust him, he'll be
capable of horrible things. I already explained the contents of every
bottle to him and showed him the ones with red labels that have the
word POISON on them."

Oh my God, I don't lock the medicine cabinet, and I do it on purpose so that Claudio can learn to repress his instincts, if it's true he's
a criminal. The other night, during dinner, my husband sent him to
the attic to get the box where he keeps his tools. My husband enjoys
carpentry. Since the boy didn't come back quickly enough, he went up
to the attic to spy on him. Claudio, according to what my husband
said, was sitting on the floor, playing with the tools, drilling a hole in
the cover of the shiny wooden box my husband so prized. Furious, he
gave him a beating right then and there. He dragged him by his ear
down to the table. My husband has no imagination. When dealing
with a boy we suspect to be abnormal, how dare he inflict a punishment on him that would have infuriated even me? We continued our
dinner in silence. Claudio, as usual, bid us good night, and when we
were alone, my husband told me: "If that monster doesn't leave this
house soon, I'm going to die."

"How impatient you are," I answered. "I'm doing an act of charity.
You must recognize that."

And to impress him still more, I invoked Your name. Before going

to bed, we always take sleeping pills from one of the containers in the
medicine cabinet, since both of us suffer from insomnia: he because
he can't sleep and rustles the book or the newspaper he's reading, or
with the cigarette he lights, and I because I hear him and start waiting
for him to fall asleep, afraid of not falling asleep myself. He had the
same idea the doctor had: that I should lock the medicine cabinet. I
didn't pay any attention to him, as I insist that trust is the means to
achieve the best results. My husband doesn't agree. For the last few
days he has become apprehensive. He says that the coffee has a strange
taste and that after he drinks it he feels dizzy, something that never
happened to him before. To reassure him I lock the medicine cabinet
when he's home. Then I open it up again. Many of my friends no
longer come over: I can't let them come, since I've told no one my
secret, except for the doctor, and You, Who know all. Nevertheless I'm
not sad. I know one day I'll have my reward and that day I will be happy again, as I was when I was single and lived next to Palermo Park, in
a little house that no longer exists except in my memory. It's all so
strange, oh my God, what's happening to me now. I would prefer
never to leave this church and could almost say that I anticipated that
feeling, since I have some candies in my purse that I brought so as not
to faint from hunger. Lunchtime has already passed and I haven't had
a bite to eat since seven this morning. You'll not be offended, oh my
God, if I have one of the candies. I am not gluttonous; you know I'm a
bit anemic and that chocolate gives me courage. I don't know why I am
afraid that something has happened in my house: I have premonitions. Those ragged ladies with black hats and feathers, and the priest
who went into the confessional, serve as omens for me. Has anyone
ever hidden in one of Your confessionals? It's the ideal place for a
child to hide. And don't I resemble a child at such moments as these?
When the priest and the ladies covered with feathers come out I'll
open the little door of the confessional and go inside. I will not confess to a priest but to You. And I will spend the whole night in Your
company. Oh my God, I know You will reward the good deeds of Your
servant.

Leopoldina's Dream

Ever since Leopoldina was born, all the women in the Yapurra family have been given names that start with L, and I, since I am so little, am called Changuito.

Ludovica and Leonor, who are the youngest ones, waited for a miracle, by the stream, every evening at dusk. We would go to the spring called Agua de la Salvia. We would leave the water jars by the spring, sit down on a rock, and wait for nightfall, our eyes wide open. All our conversations were about the same subject.

"Juan Mamanis must be in Catamarca," Ludovica would say.

"Oh. What a pretty bicycle he had! He visits the Virgin of the Valley every year."

"Would you make a vow to go on foot, like Javiera?"

"I have tender feet."

"If only we had a Virgin like that one!"

"Then Juan Mamanis wouldn't go to Catamarca."

"I'm not concerned about that. The Virgin is what worries me."

I never could sit still; they knew my habits. "Changuito, leave that alone," Ludovica would say to me, "spiders are poisonous," or "Changuito, don't do that. Don't pee in the spring."

Someone, perhaps the witch doctor, had told them that at a certain hour a light shone on the hollow amidst the stones and that a shadow appeared on the bank of the stream.

"One day we'll find her," Leonor would say. "She must look like the Virgin of the Valley."

"It might be a ghost," Ludovica would answer. "I don't have any illusions," she would say, sinking her feet in the stream and in the process sprinkling water in my eyes and ears. I was trembling. "What will you do, Changuito, when snow falls, when all the trees and the ground are white? You won't go away from the edge of the hearth, will you? Even warm water makes you tremble like a star."

"If we discover a new Virgin we'll be in the papers. They'll say this: 'Two girls in Chaquibil witnessed the apparition of a new Virgin. The highest authorities will be present at the tribute to them.' They'll build an illuminated grotto for the statue and later on there'll be a basilica. I can imagine the Virgin of Chaquibil very clearly: dark, with a scarlet gown, glasses, and a blue mantle hemmed in gold."

"I would be happy if she had on a skirt like ours and a kerchief in her hair, so long as she gave us presents."

"Virgins don't give presents or dress the way we do."

"You always think you're right."

"When I'm right, I do."

"When agreeing with you, one can't even say 'This is what I think,'" Leonor commented, stroking me on the head.

Suddenly night fell, with a smell of mint and rain.

Ludovica and Leonor filled the water jars, drank some water and went home. On the way they stopped to speak with an old man who was carrying a sack. They spoke about the long-awaited miracle. They said that at night they heard the apparition calling them. The old man replied: "It must be the fox singing. Why look for miracles away from home, when you have Leopoldina, who works miracles with her dreams?"

Ludovica and Leonor asked themselves if that was true.

In the kitchen, on a high-backed wicker chair, Leopoldina was sitting, smoking. She was so old that she looked like a scribble; you couldn't see her eyes or her mouth. She smelled like earth, grass, dry leaves: not like a person. She announced storms and good weather like a barometer; even before I did, she smelled the mountain lion coming down from the hills to eat the young goats or twist the necks of the colts. In spite of the fact that for thirty years she hadn't left the house, she knew, as birds know, where there were ripe nuts, figs, and peaches, in what valley, beside which stream. Even the crispin bird, with its sad song, as shy as a fox, came down one day to eat cracker crumbs dipped in milk from her hands, no doubt believing that she was a bush.

Leopoldina dreamed, sitting in the wicker chair. Sometimes, when she awoke, she would find the objects that had appeared in her dreams on her lap or next to the chair leg. Her dreams, however, were so modest, so poor—dreams about thorns, about stones, about branches, about feathers—that no one was surprised by the miracle.

"What did you dream of, Leopoldina?" Leonor asked, that night, when she came in.

"I dreamed that I was walking along a dry stream bed, picking up round pebbles. Here's one of them," Leopoldina said, with her flute-like voice.

"And how did you get the pebble?"

"Just by looking at it," she answered.

Beside the spring, Leonor and Ludovica no longer waited for night to come, as they had other afternoons, with the hope of witnessing a miracle. They went home, with hurried steps.

"What did you dream of, Leopoldina?" asked Ludovica.

"Of the feathers of a ringdove, which was falling to earth. Here's one of them," Leopoldina added, showing her a little feather.

"Tell me, Leopoldina, why don't you dream of other things?" asked Ludovica, impatiently.

"Honey, what do you want me to dream of?"

"Of precious stones, of rings, of necklaces, of bracelets. Of something that's good for something. Of automobiles."

"Honey, I don't know."

"What don't you know?"

"What those things are. I'm about a hundred and twenty and I've always been very poor."

"It's time to get rich. You can bring wealth to this household."

The next several days Leonor and Ludovica sat next to Leopoldina, watching her sleep. Every little while they would wake her up.

"What were you dreaming?" they would ask. "What were you dreaming?"

Sometimes she answered that she had dreamt of feathers, sometimes of pebbles, and sometimes of grass, branches, or frogs. Ludovica and Leonor protested, sometimes bitterly, other times tenderly, trying to move her, but Leopoldina did not own her dreams: they bothered her so much that she could not sleep. They decided to give her a stew that would be hard to digest.

"A heavy stomach makes you sleepy," said Ludovica, preparing a dark fritter that smelled wonderful.

Leopoldina ate, but was not sleepy.

"We'll give you some wine," said Ludovica. "Warm wine."

Leopoldina drank it, but did not fall asleep.

Leonor, who was shrewd, went to the folk healer for some soporific herbs. The healer lived in a very remote place. We had to cross the swamp, and one of the mules sank in. The herbs Leonor got from her were just as ineffective as everything else. For several days Ludovica and Leonor discussed where they should go looking for a doctor: whether to Tafí del Valle or Amaicha.

"If we go to Amaicha we can bring home grapes," Leonor said to Leopoldina, to console her. "But it's not grape season."

"And if we go to Tafí del Valle, we will get a cheese at the cheese factory at Churqui," said Ludovica.

"Why don't you take Changuito, so he can get out of the house?" Leopoldina answered, as if she didn't like cheese or grapes.

We went to Tafí del Valle. We rode slowly on horseback across the swamp where the mule had died. At the town we went to the hospital and Leonor went looking for the doctor. We waited for her on the terrace. While Leonor was speaking with the doctor, we had time to take a walk around town. When we returned Leonor was waiting for us at the hospital entrance with a package in her hand. The package contained some medicine, a syringe and needle for giving shots. Leonor knew how to give shots: a nurse she had known had taught her the art of sticking the needle in an orange or an apple. We spent the night at Tafí del Valle and the next morning, very early, set out on our way home.

When Leopoldina saw us come back, she said she was very tired, as if she had made the trip, and slept for the first time after twenty days of insomnia.

"What a scoundrel," Ludovica said. "She sleeps to show us her contempt."

As soon as they saw her waking up they asked her, "What did you dream of? You must tell us what you dreamed."

Leopoldina stammered a few words. Ludovica shook her by the arm.

"If you don't tell us your dream, Leonor will give you a shot," she added, showing her the syringe and the needle.

"I dreamed that a dog was writing my story: here it is," Leopoldina said, showing several sheets of wrinkled, dirty paper. "Won't you read them out loud, my dears, so that I can listen to them?"

"Can't you dream about more important things?" said Leonor indignantly, throwing the sheets on the ground. Then she brought a huge book that smelled like cat piss, with colour plates, that the teacher had lent her. After carefully looking through it, she paused over several of the plates, which she showed Leopoldina, rubbing them with her index finger. "Automobiles," she said, then, turning the page, "necklaces," another page, "bracelets," she blew on the pages, "jewels," she wet her finger with a drop of spit, "clocks," they turned the pages with their fingers. "These are the things you have to dream about, not all that junk."

It was at that moment, Leopoldina, that I spoke to you, but you didn't hear me, because you were sleeping again and something had changed from the time of your last dream to this one.

"Do you remember my ancestors? If you see them in me—big-bellied, rude, hot-blooded and trembling—you will remember the most sumptuous objects you ever saw: that medallion, covered with gold plate, with a lock of hair inside, which you got for your wedding; the stones of your mother's necklace, which your daughter-in-law stole; that box full of aquamarine pendants, the sewing machine, the clock, the carriage drawn by horses so old they were docile. It seems incredible, but all that existed once. Do you remember the dazzling shop in Tafí del Valle where you bought a clasp with a picture of a dog that resembled me, carved in a stone? Only I can remind you of it, to cure you of your asthma, for I was the wrap for your breast."

"If you don't sleep we'll give you a shot," threatened Ludovica.

Terrified, Leopoldina went back to sleep. Rocking back and forth, the wicker chair made a strange noise.

"I wonder if there are thieves," said Leonor.

"There's no moon."

"It must be the spirits," answered Leonor.

"Did you know why I was crying? Because I felt the hot wind blowing from the Andes."

Neither Leonor nor Ludovica could hear it, because their voices resonated so much. Desperate, or perhaps hopeful, they asked: "What did you dream? What did you dream?"

This time Leopoldina went out without answering, and said to me: "Let's go, Changuito; it's time."

Right at that moment the hot wind started blowing. In former days it had always made itself known to Christians in advance, with a very clear sky, a pale, clearly outlined sun, and a threatening noise like the sea (which I have never seen) in the distance. But this time it arrived like lightning, swept the patio, piled up leaves and branches in the hollows of the hills, beheaded the animals against the rocks, destroyed the harvest. A whirlwind swept Leopoldina and me up into the air: I, her lap dog, named Changuito, who wrote this story during my mistress's next-to-last dream.

Translator's Note

The stories in this volume were chosen from four of Silvina Ocampo's books: *Autobiografía de Irene* (Buenos Aires: Sur, 1948), *La Furia* (Buenos Aires: Sur, 1959), *Las invitadas* (Buenos Aires: Losada, 1961) and *Los días de la noche* (Buenos Aires: Sudamericana, 1970). "The Autobiography of Irene" is the title story of *Autobiografía de Irene*. "The Fury," "The Photographs," "The Clock House," "Mimoso," "The Velvet Dress," "The Objects," "Azabache," "Friends," "The House of Sugar," "The Wedding," "Voice on the Telephone," "The Sibyl," "Report on Heaven and Hell," "The Punishment," "The Basement," "Magush," "The Prayer" and "Leopoldina's Dream" are from *La Furia*. "Thus Were Their Faces," "Lovers," "Revelation," "The Bed," "The Perfect Crime," "Visions," "Icera," "The Mortal Sin," "The Expiation," and "The Guests" are from *Las invitadas*. "Livio Roca," "The Doll" and "Carl Herst" are from *Los días de la noche*.

P E N G U I N · S H O R T · F I C T I O N

Other Titles In This Series